The Collection:

Flash Fiction for Flash Memory

In Praise of *The Collection: Flash Fiction for Flash Memory*

"Remember the View-Master? Putting in the disk of pictures and pushing the lever? Each click revealed a new world. Flash Fiction for Flash Memory's vignettes capture flashbulb moments of revenge or love, sadness or wonder. *Click!* The flare of excitement as your high school crush notices you? *Click!* The icy rage of a beloved's secret life in someone else's photographs. Between each story is the delicious anticipation of what the next click will bring."

—Brian W. Sturm, Storyteller

"It's said that good things come in small packages...here's proof. These small stories linger large...for reading, discussing, remembering."

—Ruth Moose, Award-winning novelist and short story writer

"For most of human history, stories were shared aloud —in this collection, we are invited to regain that intimate space where speaker and listener shape a story into life. These flash fictions are like a Polaroid image, swiftly appearing before our eyes, a moment caught and made more precious by sharing."

—Valerie Nieman, author of *Hotel Worthy* and LifeVerse Instructor

"When my memory starts to fail me, I want to be reminded—as *Flash Fiction for Flash Memory* does so well—of how it feels to be touched by a good story. To break through the cobwebs in my mind and travel to places near and far, if just for a moment. Where paragraphs teach lessons and unite families. Where sentences evoke magic. And where hope and love are the four-letter words that matter the most."

—Landis Wade, author of *The Christmas Redemption*.

"Peer through the window into a world of emotions. From the aching loss on a one-lane bridge to the tangled memories that fill an empty box, each story in this collection leads you step by step through heartache and hope, until you realize that you're not looking through a window at all, but into a mirror."

—Monica Sanchez, PhD, Co-editor, *Storytelling: Interdisciplinary and Intercultural Perspectives*.

The Collection:

Flash Fiction for Flash Memory

Anne Anthony and Cathleen O'Connor, PhD

DEDICATION

We dedicate this book to Irene McCandless Anthony.
Daughter, sister, wife, mother, and teacher. She instilled
the love of reading by example and ended her last chapter
on earth with loving grace and a twinkle in her eye.

ACKNOWLEDGMENTS

We are deeply grateful to the authors and photographers who accepted our challenge to give us stories that thrill us, romance us, and make us laugh out loud. Special thanks to the late Marilyn Penrod for our cover image.

We are also thankful for all those who supported this project. Anne's daughters, Samantha and Jen, rallied behind her vision for this book; her sister, Mary, kept alive the spirit of their mother throughout the project; her brothers, Joe, Bill, John, and Michael, cheered her on; and her husband, Ron Puchala, every day in his wise and wonderful way kept her moving forward.

Cathleen's fellow women writers from the International Women's Writing Guild (IWWG) responded to the call for stories and offered the support of their organization to the project. Cathleen is extremely grateful to her sister writers for their contributions and encouragement. Cathleen also acknowledges her niece Caitlin who inspired her flash fiction piece about a little girl wrapped in the magic of childhood.

Every one of them brought the spirit of *The Collection* to life.

TABLE OF CONTENTS

LIST OF PHOTOGRAPHS

PREFACE

"Until I feared I would lose it, I never loved to read.
One does not love breathing."
—Harper Lee, *To Kill a Mockingbird*

In her novel, *To Kill A Mockingbird*, Harper Lee's
character, Scout talks about losing the privilege of
reading when Miss Caroline forbids her from reading
with her father Atticus. Like Scout, my mother took for
granted the pleasure of reading. She raised six children
who were constantly underfoot, but when she read she'd
lose herself to different worlds, one without dirty diapers,
a messy kitchen, and piles of laundry. She'd always have
her 'nose in a book' as my father would say and truly I
can't recall not seeing her reading something in the
evening after she finished grading papers, planning her
lesson for the next day and helping with homework. My
mother was a teacher and by her example taught her
children to love reading.

Imagine then, her consternation when her memory
began to fail her in her early seventies. During one visit, I
noticed she had switched from reading novels to
collections of short stories. When I asked about the
change, she laughed.

"Well, I can remember the plot of a short story long enough to finish." Toward the end of her life, my mother had the *ability* to read, but could no longer retain the memory of the narrative.

This collection is intended to be read by adults with memory loss who love to read. The flash fiction pieces are short enough for them to recall and enjoy. Later, friends and loved ones can use the book as a conversation starter. My mother often struggled with conversations, starting a topic, but forgetting mid-thought what she wanted to express. In those moments of frustration, I'd tell her about a time from her past as if it were a story. My storytelling would amuse her by distracting her from that moment of frustration. These flash fiction pieces can be enjoyed much the same way.

—Anne Anthony

INTRODUCTION

We set out to create an anthology for adults who struggled with memory loss. Such loss affects all aspects of a person's daily life from simple acts like finding misplaced car keys to more complex ones like reading a favorite author's latest novel.

But as we read the stories selected for the anthology, we discovered that anyone who loves the art of storytelling would enjoy them. And, more importantly, we uncovered the gift in creating something that friends and family could read to their loved ones with impaired memory.

The truth is we all have flash memory. As we move through our busy lives, finding the time to read longer narratives can be a challenge. These shorter fiction pieces between 500 and 750 words offer a flash of story to enjoy and the opportunity to connect and share with friends and family members of all ages.

Storytelling is an ancient art. Stories preserve our history and serve to teach important lessons of empathy, resilience, and wisdom. The stories we selected offer a shared world view in which characters express hope and forgiveness. You'll meet characters who despite their life circumstances reached higher and set their own course.

Other characters will influence your thinking about people and situations in different ways and perhaps inspire and change you. And, of course, there are some stories that will intrigue, shock and perhaps mystify you.

Reading aloud is often the first experience of story; parents tuck children beneath their covers, scooch beside them on the bed, and crack open the book. The sound of a parent's voice carries a child to faraway lands inhabited by dragons and noble knights and brave princesses and stirs the imagination. The sleepy child may hear the lulling cadence of 'once upon a time,' but not make it to the 'happily ever after' conclusion, drifting to sleep in comfort, in gentle reverie.

What we learned as our own family members aged and their memories declined was how to live in the moment. Talking about the past frustrates a person who cannot recall the events described. Talking about the future— something as simple as the menu for the evening dinner —would often be forgotten in minutes. We only have this moment in time to share and what better way to spend the present than to share stories.

We ask you to cozy up in a chair, bend open the book, begin at the beginning or start anywhere. Read. Out loud. Give it heart. Give it verve. Give it your all. Connect for a few minutes or an hour or more through storytelling. Return to those cherished memories of the sound of someone's voice reading. Do it for yourself or share it with someone you love.

Take a moment to look deeply at the evocative photographs included throughout the book. Images touch the mind and heart where words can't reach. Use this book to connect, converse, share and reflect.

Most importantly, be entertained.

Enjoy!

—Anne & Cathleen

Angel © Christine Paris

Sharon Bader

On An Angel Falling to Earth

(After *It Had Wings* by Alan Gurganus)

He tells the story this way: Imagine any rural homestead where the beehives sit in neat rows at the edge of the lawn. Think of an older man by the hives, wearing stained white coveralls, padded gloves and a safari hat hung with netting. A shrieking sound, as from an approaching siren, distracts him as he pulls a honey frame from a beehive at the end of a row. The sound ends in a sudden thump, clang, and groan.

"I'll be derned," he says. Tangled within his wife's clothesline, the satellite-dish-on-a-pole kind, is an angel. Nude. Definitely female, with a Rubenesque physique. The angel is translucent but for shafts of red, orange and yellow that seem to end in torn aluminum foil. The rays flash in the sunlight like a broken prism on a string as she dangles in a warm breeze. He notices her wings, crumpled where the clothesline rope pinches them, featherless holes where the metal supports punctured them. Feathers float around her as if gravity forgot its duty. She's petite and wounded and helpless.

As he lumbers across the lawn to rescue her, he pulls off hat and gloves and lets them drop to the grass. Tenderly he releases her wings and sits her on the birdbath. He kneels beside her, unsure of what to do next. She sighs and speaks to him in a voice like a violin string pitched too sharp. He clasps a hand over his nearest ear, wincing.

"Sorry," she whispers. She rubs the crest of one wing before speaking again. "I harmonize with the Hosanna Chorus, singing the highest notes of the heavenly scales. We've been practicing a new spiritual, a rather difficult piece. When our conductor told us to take five, one of those meaty basses knocked into my pedestal. Before I could break my fall, I slipped through a storm cloud and struck a bolt of lightning."

He shakes his head in wonder.

"I've sheared my upper prism notes and lost my blue notes." She leans her head closer to his. "For me, blue notes carry longing. They balance my vocal spectrum."

"Never could carry a tune," he says, running his fingers through thinning gray hair. "But I think I can help you."

He retrieves a beehive frame and brushes away possessive bees with a goose wing feather. He sits on the grass next to the birdbath and stands the frame in his lap.

"Honey heals," he tells her. He puddles his fingers in

the spaces of the honeycomb. "My bees make blue honey that's nothin' short of miraculous." He daubs the honey on her wings while he speaks in a low and soothing voice. As he works she begins to hum and her wings plump with supple feathers. His fingers begin to tingle and then his arms and whole body. A lightness overturns the darker side of his spirit like soil hoed in a spring garden. He finishes her transformation by double checking for any rogue rays of colored light. He feels breezy flutters as she tests her wings.

She floats to the ground and he hears a "thank you" in a soft marbled trill. She ascends skyward, a ray of pure white light backlit by slow moving thunderclouds. They're gone far eastward before he realizes the beehive frame still hangs from his hand and he walks with a light step to the beehives. He wonders if his wife noticed the angel's presence from their kitchen windows.

"I've a mind not to tell her," he says to the bees.

Sharon Bader has had a longstanding love affair with reading and writing. She cut her literary teeth writing poetry and published regularly in school newspapers and journals. Lately, she concentrates on producing short fiction and nonfiction pieces with a publishing credit in the second *Sisters in Crime* anthology.

Alice Benson
Computer Dating

R obert stood outside the Senior Center, trying not to feel old. At seventy-one, he was active and energetic, an avid hiker and gardener. He didn't often think of himself as a senior, but he came to the Center, because it was a good place to learn more about his computer. When his daughter moved six hundred miles away, she kept telling him how much easier it would be to keep in touch if he was "on line." He bought a new computer, and after a month of practice, he was pretty good with email and loved the instant photos of his grandsons, but he wanted to learn more.

His daughter even suggested he use the computer for dating, reminding him that, "Mom's been gone for over five years." He just laughed at the notion of finding love using a machine.

"If I get interested in another woman it will be because I see something in her face. You can't tell anything from a written description. As soon as I saw your mother's eyes, I knew I would marry her." Robert wasn't interested in dating. He filled his life with activity and didn't consider the possibility of loving again.

He took a seat toward the back and watched the room fill up, waiting for the teacher, probably some twenty-year old. Robert's guess was confirmed when a young man walked to the front of the room.

"Good morning. I'm here to get you started. Please take a moment to turn on your computers." He demonstrated. Robert found the button without any trouble and helped the man sitting on his right.

The door opened, and an attractive woman close to Robert's age walked to the front. She addressed the class.

"Sorry to be late. I'm Lois Adams, your instructor." She turned to the young man. "Thank you for getting everything set up." He nodded and left the room. Lois' voice was musical, her smile warm.

She turned to the class. "Welcome to Basic Computers. I see you have your terminals turned on, so let's get started." Lois spent a few minutes going through some fundamentals related to Internet browsers, search engines, and email. Robert followed her instructions with no problems. The man on his right kept poking Robert's arm and asking for help, which Robert was happy to supply.

"Now let's try a little more hands-on experience." Lois put a short exercise on the screen. "Just follow the instructions, and raise your hand if you have questions."

She walked around the room, assisting as needed.

Robert finished the work and turned to help his neighbor. Lois nodded approval. He noticed her beautiful blue eyes and silvery curls and was surprised to feel his heart hammer in his chest. He hadn't felt like this in many years. He also shocked himself by noting that her left hand was ring-free. He turned back to his computer, feeling a bit bewildered, and suddenly grateful he had decided to take this course.

Lois led the students through one more lesson. As Robert watched her, he saw again how attractive she was. His hands were suddenly sweaty and his mouth dry. Maybe he was wrong about not wanting to date.

After Lois dismissed the class, Robert took his time gathering his papers as well as gathering his nerve. He walked to the front of the room where Lois was focused on the computer.

"Excuse me."

"Yes?" Lois looked up at Robert. The skin around her eyes crinkled as she smiled. "Thank you for everything today. I can't always get to everyone's questions, and when you assisted the person next to you, I was able to help others. Maybe you should take the advanced class next time."

Robert felt himself flush. His brown eyes looked into her clear blue ones, and he felt himself floating away.

This was his opportunity, but he couldn't make his voice cooperate. Did he really want to do this?

"I'm glad I was able to help," Robert said in a rush, then stopped, unsure again.

"There's a great little sandwich shop just a block away." Lois' eyes sparkled. "It's almost noon, and I'm starved." She paused, smiling at him.

She was smart, funny, and gorgeous. Robert's reluctance disappeared. "Me, too. How about having lunch together?"

"I'd love to." Lois took his arm as they walked out of the classroom, and Robert almost laughed out loud, thinking how he'd tell his daughter about his experience with computer dating.

Alice Benson has been published in several literary journals including a 2016 Main Street Rag Anthology. Her first novel, *Her Life is Showing*, set in a domestic violence shelter, was inspired by her work in the human services field. She recently retired and lives in Wisconsin with her partner and their two dogs.

Visit her at www.alicebensonauthor.com.

Kathryn Harless
A Good Left Hook

The clock over the kitchen sink read 11:35 pm. It was the middle of February. Sarah sat on the bench outside the front door of her duplex watching the warmth of her breath billow out into small makeshift clouds. Snow trickled down and landed on her bare feet. She was still in shock after what had transpired moments earlier.

Dumbfounded.

There were no tears, no need for them. The evening was a culmination of years of betrayal that had reached a crest. An awakening brought on by a lifetime of crying out, only to be hit square in the face by dead silence. Inside balloons hung languidly from the ceiling, their colorful tails trailing to the confetti strewn floor. The banner celebrating her daughter's second birthday still taped over the entrance of the dining room. In their sparse living room, the rocking horse Sarah gave her was her child's new best friend.

The evening began in the same manner as the day started out: a slam of the front door from her husband signaling their argument can pick up where they left it that morning. Anything and everything was fodder for a knock-down-drag-out fight. One that usually ended in bruises and a trip to the ER.

However, this fight didn't have the typical trademarks of an "all-nighter." The evening dragged its heels until Sarah put their little girl down for the night. A few well-chosen words on her part and they were back in their appointed corners with the kid-gloves off. Bedtime came, and she wanted to get one final jab in. A jab to the groin, so to speak, that would render him speechless and one that the marriage could not recover from.

The water swirled around the bowl as Sarah held the handle down, hoping the gold band would get flushed away along with her marriage. The door locked; her husband banged on the thin piece of wood that separated them. He yelled, "How dare you," and a string of threats that kept her barricaded in the bathroom.

With the familiar slam of the front door and the sound of Sarah's daughter crying from her nursery, she opened the door and ran to her child's side. Sarah held her tight against her as she tip-toed down the hall, checking to see if he was still in the house. The coast clear, she locked the door, grabbed a chair from the dining room and shoved it under the doorknob for added security. After putting her daughter back into her crib, Sarah called her parents, hoping Dad would pick up the phone instead of

Mom. They never did see eye-to-eye on, well, anything really. Dad was a safe bet to come to her rescue.

The TV blared in the background as Dad yelled "Mary, turn the sound down, I'm on the phone."

"Dad, Dad...he left," Sarah said, more matter of fact, then a tear laden sob of regret. Dad muffled the receiver with his hand, but she could still make out his words, "Bill left Sarah." Not expecting a reply from Mom, he removed his hand and was about to speak.

"Good, I'm glad he left that bitch!"

Sarah recalled asking her dad to come over and him whispering that he would, "Call you from work tomorrow."

The rest of the phone conversation was a blur. Her mind stuck on the fact her mother called her a bitch and blatantly took her son-in-law's side. And that's how Sarah ended up on the front porch, in shock. Even though she did not know for certain the whereabouts of her husband, it was a safe bet that he was in the loving arms of *his* parents and sister.

For well over 35 years **Kathern Harless** has lived in Memphis, TN with her teenage son and foxhound pup. Ms. Harless' writing tends to lean towards the human condition. She has the uncanny ability to make your heart swell, shatter, and melt the tiny shards with the stroke of her pen.

"Once you learn to read,
you will be forever free."
— Frederick Douglass

Lost Highway © Rollin Jewett

Jane Shlensky
Round Trips

He drives long-distance semis, days alone, picking up hitchers like me on the road. He seems to live on coffee, mints, and cake he buys at truck stops where he laughs and flirts with waitresses and hollers at the cooks. He's thin as a tire iron but somehow looks so tough and wary, who would ever guess he has advice to give, amends to make. He promises a ride to Abilene so I have hours to nap or hear him talk. He takes to me as if I am a wheel he feels obliged to steer along the road.

A job like this must make him lonely, wild for company of any scroungy kind. He knows me at a glance, it seems, for his eyes scan me like radar looking for my faults, what could have put me traveling on my thumb. His gravelly voice is kind. He needs an ear, small thanks for me to pay him for the ride. He drives and thinks aloud, an easy pace.

"You make enough mistakes, you learn some tricks to traveling light or learning to forgive. Although some folks with feelings hard as stone like to snap whips, see blood, pile error on. Punishing minds can stay too close to home. Regret and shame get heavy, backs can't lift so hard a load; you have to set it down. You shed your sins like snakes slough summer skins. You laugh at insults, mostly 'cause they're true, control your temper. You have to own your faults."

He's busy knocking memory's doors, half hoping they're unlocked by one inside his thoughts, but half afraid of curtains closed on faces that he knew once but no more. He drives and waits at doors, his hat in hand.

"Whew! Damn," he says, half shaking off a ghost. "You eat some crow, some humble pie, some shit, and try to put down roots. You try to please, but highways sing like the Sirens in that poem and soon you have to go no matter what. The ones you leave don't see Odysseus when you come back, I tell you that for sure."

He laughs, and I do too, a bit surprised that he reads Homer. There my misjudgment shows. I wonder just what other things he knows, Bhagavad-Gita stuffed beside his maps.

"Do you have folks, a wife and kids?" I ask. He smiles with sad acceptance.

"Used to have. I couldn't live a sedentary way. My stories longed for a far place I'd traveled with a pack or on the job. But there are other walkers on this road," he says, suggesting me, "good company who know this lay of land and travel light as rain. Their stories keep me up many a night, as mine do them, unless my guess is wrong." He lifts his eyebrows up; I nod.

It's true. He has to know he's in my head, his story bound with mine. I feel him stare, as if he reads my mind.

"You'll be just fine, son. Sometimes it works out."

I sit in silence, watching the road subside. I dream of the door I need to open, hoping with all I am I have the grace to accept the blame I'm due. I dream their eyes smile, surprised and glad to see me. I dream they take my hand and pull me in. I dream I'm changed, and get life right this time.

Jane Shlensky, veteran teacher and musician, has recent poetry in a number of literary journals and anthologies. The North Carolina Poetry Society nominated her poem, *Insomnia*, for a 2017 Pushcart Prize, their second nomination of her poetry, and three of her short fiction pieces were contest finalists. Jane's chapbook *Barefoot on Gravel* (2016) is available from Finishing Line Press. Find her online: http://www.writersdigest.com/whats-new/write-poetry-jane-shlensky.

Ashley Memory
The Dave Department

"Mrs. Herbert Sinclair?" said the man at her door. "I'm Dave." Eloise was so flabbergasted she didn't know what to say. The man, in his early thirties, wearing tan shorts and a blue T-shirt, seemed happy to be there. He had curly brown hair and steady hazel eyes.

"I'm sorry, I, I didn't expect you so soon."

Then she realized that he could have been there for any number of reasons. Ever since Herb died, she found herself the victim of a thousand little catastrophes. Her late husband had had the nerve, God bless him, to deny her the gallantry of a protracted illness but instead falling dead of a sudden heart attack on a Saturday morning— the same day two cubic yards of mulch were delivered to their house!

She was now also in charge of getting her internet connection fixed so she could get emails from her sons in Cincinnati and Knoxville. And then there was the washing machine…. Her week had begun with a flurry of phone calls, and it seemed that her destiny was in the hands of countless men named Dave who were always at lunch. None of them had even called her back! The young man sensed her frustration.

"At your service, Ma'am." His voice was so kind she wanted to throw her arms around him in relief. Instead, she stood there and watched, amazed.

First, without even being directed, he went to the kitchen and examined the wall behind the little table that served as her study. He looked around the computer and pulled out a little white box.

"Here is your modem," he said. "It looks like the cable came loose." He reattached it and moved away so she could sit down. "See if the connection is restored." And it was.

"Now," he said, "wasn't there also something wrong with your washing machine?"

"This way," she said, leading him down to the basement. She pointed toward her white 1982 Roper.

"Might take me a little longer on this one. Let's turn it on." The machine began as usual but once it filled with water, it stopped.

"This is where the trouble begins," she said. "It won't go to the next cycle."

"Not anymore," he said. "Give me a minute. I'm going back to the van." He returned minutes later with a part in his hand. Next, she heard her washing machine draining and spinning happily.

"Done!" he said triumphantly, bounding up the stairs. "All you needed was a new timer."

"I'm impressed. Would you like a glass of orangeade?"

"Not yet," he said. "There's a big load of mulch in your front yard. Would you like me to spread it for you?"

"Yes, yes," she said, still in shock. Had she even called about the mulch? Yet she didn't dare say anything. This was going to cost a fortune, but she didn't care. From her window, she watched as he heaved shovel after shovel of pine bark. Then he mounded it neatly around her roses with his bare hands.

"What's wrong?" he asked, as he jogged up the front steps. "You're crying."

"You can't imagine what I've been through. All the run-arounds, all the phone messages. All the Daves. Before I met you, I had decided that everybody named Dave was trouble."

He grinned, taking the glass of orangeade she held in her shaking hand. "You've got to understand something. The other Daves in the world are not always where they need to be. Those of us in the Dave Department are works in progress. You've got to be patient with us."

"Is there really a Dave Department?"

He laughed. "Not really. It just sounded good."

"I've been unfair, I know. I've judged harshly."

"It's okay. We all do it." He handed her the empty glass. Then his cell phone beeped. "Gotta go. Another service call."

"But wait. What about the bill?"

"Forget about it," he said, flicking his hand. "It's been a pleasure. Have a nice day."

As he drove away, Eloise she realized that she didn't get his last name. How would she ever thank him? Later that day, she drew up a list of all the companies she'd ever called. She started with Uwharrie Telecommunications. "I, uh, need to leave a message for Dave."

"Which one?" asked the woman on the phone. "Dave Holloway? Or Dave Milligan?"

"Both," said Eloise. "Both of them. Just to be safe."

Ashley Memory writes fiction, essays, and poetry. Her work has appeared in *The Thomas Wolfe Review*, *Wildlife in North Carolina*, *Romantic Homes*, *Brilliant Flash Fiction*, *The Naugatuck Review*, and *The Gyroscope Review*. Her work is forthcoming in the annual baseball review, *The Hardball Times*.

Snowy Egret © Jennifer Puchala

Anne Anthony
The Selfie

The ding or ping or whatever you want to call the irritating noise discharged from Margie's cellphone lying next to her wine glass on the table. I'd spent weeks arranging and rearranging our hectic schedules for this girls' night out and now her daughter's constant texting kept interrupting our conversation. Margie picked up her phone, adjusted her reading glasses, and peered down. She laughed.

"Another selfie?" I asked although I knew her answer. She turned the phone toward me so I could enjoy yet another selfie of her daughter. I glanced and smiled.

"Cute."

"You didn't look, Angela," she said. "Oh, what's wrong?" The sudden slack in Margie's cheeks warned me not to answer truthfully. She's one of those women who likes everyone to be happy and content.

"Nothing." I reached for my dirty martini. Her phone dinged again before I set down my glass. Margie giggled now, stood up, slid over to sit by my side to share her daughter's photo.

"Look how beautiful she is," she said, handing me her phone. "She's me without wrinkles and crow's-feet and this damn extra chin. It's as if I'm looking back in time."

I've known Margie since high school when we went everywhere together. Before school. After school. Every weekend. Now we're lucky if we get together once a year despite living thirty minutes from each other.

"She does resemble you." I leaned in for closer look. Her daughter sat on a wooden bench on a pier overlooking the ocean. "Is that Kure Beach?"

Margie nodded absorbed by her glance back in time.

"Kevin drove us there when we were first married." I said. "Almost every weekend. Even in winter."

Said he liked how the sun lit my eyes against the blue ocean waves. We hadn't been there for years. I grabbed my reading glasses, adjusted them on my nose—this latest pair pinched slightly—pulled the phone within inches of my face to assess how much the pier had changed. A patch of red in the background caught my eye. I spread my two fingers across the screen to zoom.

"I've got to go," I said, dropping the phone. Margie's mouth opened but I never heard a word she said as I raced out the door. I don't recall driving home. I know I did. How else would I be here in my home on the comfortable couch sitting with Kevin? How long I waited for his return home, I can't say.

He'd promised. The third time it happened.

"I'll never. I promise you, Angie. Mere flirtation. I swear. Meant nothing."

Of course I believed him. All wives do, well, the gullible ones. Fool me once. But three times? He denied the patch of red hair was his as he stood inches from me wearing the same damn golf shirt I'd seen on Margie's phone, in her daughter's selfie, behind her daughter's shoulder, and pressed up against a woman half his age. Their lips locked.

He denied those lips, even when I reached for the butcher's knife. If only he hadn't laughed. Lips wide open. I glanced down at Kevin now lying on the floor and checked his lips. Locked forever.

Anne Anthony has been published in the *North Carolina Literary Review, Brilliant Flash Fiction, Dead Mule School for Southern Literature, Poetry South,* and elsewhere. She holds a Masters in Professional Writing from Carnegie Mellon University. She lives and writes full-time in North Carolina. She is a member of the North Carolina Writers' Network and the International Women's Writing Guild.

Visit the author at http://anneanthony.weebly.com.

Bernadine Lortis
Okay, Okay

Crossing a tangle of railroad tracks, I speed through an industrial park maze of red brick construction, challenging every traffic light; but it's Saturday so there'll be no excuses if I'm late. I'm on a mission and I'm a man who can't keep a woman waiting, not the woman I've always loved.

I slam to a stop before a tiny lonely bungalow, the only one remaining in what was once a thriving immigrant neighborhood. A patchwork of shingles dip and slope sideways, weathered boards peal for paint and like my nearly blind grandma, the bungalow sags into the barren ground, as out of place in this land-developers' planned upscale setting as buggy whips in Detroit in its heyday. Gran refused to move to a different place—a safer place with comforts and services she deserves—but today's the day I pack her things and take her to live with me.

The whistle from her dented copper kettle greets me at the door as I knock.

"Koli, chile? Screen no-close. Okay?"

Nothing wrong with her hearing but English never

28

fully developed. She skips last consonants, like the 'd' in child and everything ends with 'Okay?' Her words drift down dark hallways, fragile as moonbeams but just as constant, something I can count on—unless thick clouds descend. We each lost a child, Gran and me. When Dad fell in Viet Nam, I broke apart clouds for her and she did the same for me after Joey's accident. The moon kept shining.

She loves vinegar, bathes in it, drinks it, softens towels, scrubs every surface she touches—you name it. When I step inside, its acrid odor mingles with scents I'll always remember. I follow my nose through stale talcum powder and dust to the sweet comfort of burnt cinnamon sugar and warm homemade rolls that tempt me from the worn, once-varnished table as I sit down.

Above it, nail holes climb cracked plaster over sepia photographs I have to keep lowering. It's like visiting nursery school twenty years ago viewing Joey's eye-level finger paintings. As Gran continued to shrink, I've emptied shelves in her cupboards and closets until now she keeps everything laid out on the counter or chests in neat stacks.

"Chile, if I can just reach…touch. No move things, okay?"

She doesn't turn as I enter. Bent nearly in half, her stooped back—tied in a tangle of apron strings that crisscross her thin house dress, its print faded long ago into a blur—hides even her topknot. Buttery streaks, one above each ear, gather into pale ribbons what remains of sparse white strands. She once owned a wig but trashed it with potato peels in the slop pail under the sink, retrieving it as a plaything for her cat to pounce on.

Her suntan disappeared when the property contractor cemented over the garden she planted to coincide with moon cycles. Wild dandelions she used for wine and salad couldn't survive commercial weed killer, but she's kept up a fierce fight to stay put. Now translucent skin droops from her miniature frame and purple veins map swollen legs and gnarled hands. I watch her fingers tremble as she pours boiling water into her pink teapot, while nudging Whiskers, the mouser, with her one good foot where bunions and hammer toes shape black high-top shoes. I don't yet dare offer to do for her what she does for herself when I'm not around. She's still the perfect hostess in ways that count to her.

"The moon, Koli—full was it, last night?" Gran asks as she peers around like a fallen bird. Cataracts cloud once startling blue eyes or I swear I could see through to her stubborn soul. She reaches out and smiles in my general direction before hobbling across the scarred linoleum with the steaming pot.

The teapot has been cracked since I was little. "Only the glaze," she'd said, "now, Koli—outsides—no matter."

To me the broken lines looked like a design of two chickens fighting. We gave them names, Jim and Jam, and made up stories about them. They always ended up friends in the end. Gran made me laugh and feel hopeful about the world.

"Oh, chile, chile," she says now, grabbing onto my shirt and belt for leverage. Her hug lasts longer than usual today. Then, retreating from our embrace, she pats my hand and kisses it in final acceptance.

"Okay, Koli," she nods, "Okay!"

Bernadine Lortis has written secretly and sporadically for years; began submitting July 2016. Fiction, creative nonfiction and poetry has been published in numerous online journals and anthologies. She lives in St. Paul, MN with her husband of 46 years near their daughter and finds inspiration and appreciation all around her.

Kendall Vanderwouw
The Case of the Missing Remote Box

ook, Charlie," Liam said, "the scene of the crime."
They stood next to the couch in our keeping room.

"What are you doing?" I asked my brother, Liam, as I walked into the room.

"Charlie and I are searching the scene of the crime for clues." He held up his teddy bear.

"Wait. What happened?" I asked, becoming genuinely scared.

"I call it, 'The Case of the Missing Remote Box.'" Liam looked back at me.

"What?" I asked. "Is the box that you made at summer camp missing?"

Liam didn't reply, he just walked in a circle around me, and whispered in my ear, "I'll find where you hid it." A classic six-and-a-half-year-old brother move: being suspicious of your older sister.

My brother was obsessed with crime movies and books. For some reason, he always pictured our family as basic characters in a crime story and I was always the villain. I tried to ignore it. Liam "searching the crime scene" happened like three times a week. He almost always ended it in Stage One. An hour or so later, I heard the click of Liam's rusty flashlight. Oh no, I thought to myself. Stage Two.

Liam loved solving crimes. I decided after a while that he always went about it the same way. He started by searching the scene. That's where most of his "cases" end. He normally found the thing he lost and forgot about it. I knew it was a big deal that we reached Stage Two.

Liam burst through my door and slammed it closed. My entire bedroom echoed. He flipped my light switch off and lit his flashlight up. I sat up in my bed. He stared at me with a serious look. How I hate Stage Two.

"So," I said, trying to break the tension, "how's things?"

Liam picked up the flashlight, and stood on his tippy toes so that he could hold it over my head.

"Ava, what did you do with the box?" he asked intensely.

Stage Two: Interrogation.

"I didn't do it, Liam. It was probably Charlie. I see the way he eyes that box."

"Ava, his eyes are made of plastic."

"I know what I saw."

Liam is six-and-a-half. How much more do I really have to say? Though for some reason, not even a six-and-a-half year-old would believe my Charlie theory. Liam stared at me in denial. Luckily, he left after I told him that I had to do homework for the rest of the night.

At nine thirty-five on Thursday night in northern Colorado, a girl, twelve-years-old with brunette hair, was caught trying to plant evidence on a teddy bear.

I could hear the headline now in my mind. Liam was long asleep; after all, he was six-and-a-half. How do you plant evidence on a bear? That's what I'd been trying to figure out for the past forty-five minutes.

Okay, he caught me. I took the box. The guilt was eating me up, even though I had a good reason for taking the box. It didn't do its job. The box fell over ten times a day, if not, more. But, I didn't want to find out what is in Stage Three.

The next morning, I woke up with a feeling of satisfaction. In my pajamas and baggy pull-over sweatshirt, I ventured to the kitchen table to get my breakfast. Someone was waiting there for me.

"Hello, Ava," Liam said as he looked at me. "Anything you want to tell me?"

"Nope," I said and reached for a banana which he

gladly grabbed away from the fruit bowl and began to eat. Stage Three was the worst stage.

"Will you excuse me?" I asked and put an anxious smile across my face.

My socks slipped on the hardwood floor as I ran to my hiding spot. First door on the right as you walked in: the coat closet. I scrambled through boxes of baby clothing only to find nothing. The box was gone. In the kitchen, the table was empty. Liam was gone. I had been played by a six-and-a-half year-old.

Stage Three: Realization.

He let that guilt tear me apart for three days, and for what? To play detective.

Kendall Vanderwouw has loved reading and writing from a very young age. She has three publications for poetry, won an essay contest about science fiction, and has won an honorable mention from a national contest for poetry. She loves writing short stories, especially about her personal experiences.

Warmest Comforts © Samantha Hess

Dori Dupré
See You in September

D emetria sat at The Soda Shoppe table, her fingers rubbing the smooth wooden tabletop nervously, right to left and right to left. It was August 31st, still a southern hot and humid summer day, and school was in its second week already. She kept her eyes cast low while watching him across the diner. He swept the floor, in quick spurts, right in rhythm to the song on the jukebox, some new song about seeing you in September. He wore a white shirt and blue apron tied neatly behind his waist. The back of his blond hair touched the bottom of his neck. Her father would not approve.

Her body braced against the booth while waiting for her friends to arrive. She was too scared to go talk to him; her heart raced even considering it. But he had winked at her during their music lesson at Mrs. Potter's house yesterday. He smiled softly at her when she sat down to play Chopin on the piano, and it made her cheeks hot, both embarrassed and excited. She liked that feeling, but it also made her feel silly. Too silly to smile back. Why didn't she smile back? She could just kick herself.

He was new to town, maybe from someplace more glamorous like Malibu, California. He kept to himself in the hallways at school and didn't seem to be loud like the other boys. He carried a notepad around, and when it wasn't stuck in his pants pocket, he'd always be scribbling inside. Demetria wondered what was he writing in there. He'd have his nose in a book, usually some novel, between classes when everyone else was trying to kiss each other and not get caught by the assistant principal.

Demetria hadn't even heard his voice. He never spoke around her. What did he sound like? Ellen and Mary Catherine had no problem talking to boys. All kinds of boys. They would know what to do. They would know what to say to this mysterious boy who took music lessons with her for the past two Tuesdays after school. This mysterious boy who swept a floor to the beat of Frankie Valli and The Four Seasons. This mysterious boy who needed a haircut.

The waitress dropped off Demetria's root beer float onto the table, and Mary Catherine skipped into the diner like a tropical breeze. Soon after, Ellen walked in like a well-mannered bolt of lightning: confident, striking, and full of loud noises as her heels clapped along the tile floor. She was clearly on a mission.

The song changed on the jukebox, prompting him to look up from his work. Eyeing Ellen, he watched her walk over to the booth and sit down. Then he looked directly at Demetria. He caught her looking at him, too. Her cheeks became hot again; her throat started to close. Then he smiled at her and walked over to the booth, broom still in hand.

"Hi, Demi."

Demetria could barely speak. "Hi." It was all she could say, barely a whisper. She wasn't even sure of his name. But he knew hers.

"I'll see you in September." He winked, and turned to walk away. His voice was older sounding, whiskey-soaked almost, just like a musician's. Was he writing songs in that little notepad he kept with him?

Her friends, with mouths wide open, watched him walk away and into the back kitchen. Mary Catherine asked, almost shouting, "Who was that?"

"He's a new boy." It was all Demetria could get out.

"How does he know you?" implored Ellen. It was clear that Demetria's friends were not going to let that brief encounter simply blow over.

Demetria leaned back into her cushion and breathed out all the air she had been holding inside ever since she saw him sweeping. All the goofy butterflies in her stomach were being set free, but they would come back as soon as he walked away.

"He takes piano with me at Mrs. Potter's. I don't even know his name."

And as Demetria tried to explain to her friends that he was new in town and school and piano lessons at Mrs. Potter's, he returned from the back kitchen with a bus pan, clearing a nearby booth of its dirty dishes. Demetria watched him make quick work of it and saw him glance over at the table of girls. She knew he could hear the girls' mumbling through the jukebox music playing in the background.

Demetria noticeably looked over at him, and when their eyes met, he smiled that same soft smile, winning her heart for at least a moment.

Dori Ann Dupré is originally from New Jersey. She is the author of the two-time award-winning novel, *Scout's Honor*, and several published short stories, poems and articles. Her second novel, *Good Buddy*, is scheduled for release in 2018. Dori works and resides in Raleigh, North Carolina.

Zachariah Claypole White
Books from Keida

The woman named Keida sent him books of poetry: sometimes Neruda, sometimes Eliot, sometimes names he did not know. Alexander read them all and sent her fiction in return: O'Connor, Steinbeck, even King. Keida once said fiction used too many words to make its point. He replied that poetry didn't use enough.

Over the years, the books arrived from a series of P.O. boxes as Keida moved from state to state, country to country, but this book would be his last. The note, stuck to a collection of Sappho's work, mixed in with the day's gardening catalogs and donation requests, said as much.

Alexander ran his fingers down the book's spine. He had hoped to find meaning in this final gift—an ending in half-remembered fragments. It seemed appropriate, but he couldn't say why. Age in a nutshell.

A familiar itch prickled beneath his wedding ring. If only he could demand to see her, speak to her one last time, but Keida had never given a home address or a phone number, and here, at the end, that would not change. It would ruin the mystery, and Keida did love a mystery. They both did—it kept things interesting. Otherwise they were two geriatric wackos sending letters that should not be sent. Had she passed already? A note received from beyond the grave, Keida would love that.

Alexander scratched through thinning hair and scanned the shelves wrapping his study walls. Many of the books were from her. Attached to each was a piece of neatly folded paper. The notes varied as much as the books— recounting jokes, losses, uncertainties, death—but always started with the same four words, igniting a heartbeat to the fragile cursive: *My Dearest Alexander Overcroft*. Never Alex, or even Alexander.

When he finished a book, he'd tape the accompanying note to the first page and place the volume on his shelf. But there would be no more books, no more names beyond his ability to pronounce, no more pages to mark with expired credit or health insurance cards. No more words from Keida.

His hands, ever steady and determined, hurled books to the floor: first one volume, then another, then two at a time. There was no anger in the movement, no emotion. No tears. After all, why mourn a stranger? He and Keida had met only once, in a bookstore that smelled of cigarettes and weed. The store was gone now, rebuilt as part of a high-rise.

Ever-growing spaces filled the shelves; books piled around him. He grabbed the buy-one-get-one-free packaging tape from his desk and searched the room for a box, a bag, a fucking garbage can. He needed to rid himself of the books. He would sell them. No, donate them, to a library, a high school, or maybe a prison. He didn't care.

If someone had glimpsed him through the window, they might have remembered roads cracking beneath last February's ice. Or they might have seen a crazy old man throwing books like wedding confetti. Alexander laughed, but the sound was static breaking across a television screen.

He stopped, swore, and picked up a collection of Seamus Heaney.

"You'd haunt me if I packed them away, wouldn't you?" Heaney's photograph stared back. "Well, fine." Alexander tossed the book to the floor. "But don't expect me to be happy about it." From his resting place by the wall, Heaney didn't say much.

Alexander reached for Sappho's work, stared at it for a moment or two, then pulled Keida's note from the cover and carefully taped it to the acknowledgments page. As he turned from the heaps of poetry, the weight of grief pushed against his failing knee.

With a groan, he flicked off the light switch, and paused. In the living room, his wife was sketching. He couldn't see her, but the sound of pencil over paper was as familiar as her snoring. Alexander stepped out and eased the door closed. Slowly, he shuffled away from the study, the letters, the books. Tomorrow he would reorganize them. *Tomorrow.*

In the darkness behind him, the cursive of the woman named Keida, whose r's looked too much like s's, filled Alexander with the ache of an August thunderstorm. Her words bled into Heaney, Sappho, Shakespeare, Bashō, and countless others, dancing between pages, caught in the knowing silence of a closed book waiting for the touch of familiar hands.

Zachariah Claypole White is a recent graduate of Oberlin College. He writes poetry, short fiction, and song lyrics. He also performs in two North Carolina-based bands, The Arcadian Project and Eden Falling. His poems have appeared in *The Plum Creek Review, The Albion Review,* and *Scalawag*, and has received numerous awards.

Mary Mullen
Table Rock Road

When they fixed Table Rock Road they left the one-lane bridge. The bridge with the knobby stone corners and the heavy stone paving and the low gothic arch where Daddy said the White River trolls hide, waiting to steal your shoes when you're wading in shallow waters. The town fixed the road up and drew nice white and yellow lines and gave it an inch of shoulder, but they left the bridge. The summer they fixed it the road was closed so we had to drive up into Missouri and down around the big bridges on the other side of the lake just to go swimming.

I'd tell my dad that I'd be home late because it took so long for Maggie to drive me home. In the afternoons, in Maggie's silver Honda, I'd see Ronnie's dad standing behind a construction sign telling us to 'stop' or 'slow' and I'd wave each time and his dad would nod, but the whole time I was cursing the summer construction and waving off Maggie's cigarette smoke and wondering if Ronnie would be at the lake too. And when the road was reopened, the bridge was like it was before, with just enough room for one little car to cross, so when the north road curved left and the south road curved right, the cars would meet, unannounced, on either side and wait to see who would go first. I told my father to fix that bridge.

"Just tear it down and make it bigger."

But he said he had his first kiss under that bridge. He said he took us kids there every Sunday after church. He said he loved the bridge and he was the mayor and there wasn't any money and no one else wanted to fix the bridge except Lanie Klien and she was from Texas and wasn't from Table Rock and so no one had to listen to her anyway.

"Besides, the trolls might move into town if we tear down that bridge." Daddy said it and that was it. Just like when he said, "Get back home by nine or else," or "Don't stay out at the lake with Ronnie."

One night I dreamt the bridge got fixed and the trolls came into town and they ran the candy store and the gas station and the grocery store, and I had to go in to get milk—like the whole world would die if I didn't get milk—and I was scared out of my mind, but everyone else was shopping like it was no big deal, and I got up to the checkout line and then I woke up in a sweat because I saw the trolls' faces in my dream.

And no one talked about fixing the bridge after the crash either. Or if they did, they did it where I couldn't hear them. Guess they didn't want me thinking about

Daddy, and his bridge, and the big black Suburban that ran his little green convertible into the river. Guess they didn't want to cause trouble. But grief doesn't cause amnesia, so I can still hear him hollering down the river from his seat on the flat rocks, "Don't get too close to that bridge, not unless you want to meet one of those White River trolls."

I'd keep going, moving from rock to rock along the banks, watching for crawdads, until my arms and legs were lined with goosebumps, each little hair standing on end like sunflowers at high noon, maybe from the cold water on my feet or the shade under the canopy of beech trees, or the light breeze that swept down from the lake and passed through the river bends, ringing the leaves on the trees like bells before hustling off to nowhere.

"They'll steal your shoes!" Then he would hiss real low, "Might even try to kiss you." But by then, I would have already turned around.

Mary Mullen is a writer and policy analyst living in Minneapolis, Minnesota. She was a finalist for the 2016 Indian Review Half K Prize, and her short essays have recently appeared in *Entropy* and *Storm Cellar*. Learn more at: marydenisemarch.wordpress.com.

Excited Dog © P. Decker

Karlee Fain

How the Brown Blur Taught the Girl to Yell at Cops and Be Less Logical in North Carolina

The story might have begun with the time Cora practiced scream therapy on a police officer. The man sloppily clad in blue government-issued polyester and black boots had earned it. It never occurred to Cora how it might have looked to her conservative southern neighbors in Greensboro, NC when a string bean shaped girl raised her voice to a man in uniform.

In a city where bitterness was sweetened like tea to sound like "bless her heart," using words directly confirmed to her neighbors that this Yankee brought with her the northern aggression that sparks wars.

"Your dog shit all over the house," was the last thing the officer said, running his fingers through greasy black hair. "And I had to clean it all up."

But the story actually starts a couple months earlier, when Cora pulled into the driveway of her first apartment. It was one of four units in a large prewar house with a shared sprawling wrap-around porch. It had been divided, like the rest of Greensboro, into smaller apartments.

Sitting on the back of the stoop was her neighbor, the officer, trying to harness a small brown blur in his hands, something that wiggled so quickly it was hard to imagine it had any defined lines.

Cora crossed from her side of the porch to his, realizing this bundle of steam was the smallest dog she'd ever seen. Libee, the size and temperament of a hamster on its wheel, spun her little legs for no gain other than forward momentum. She was equal parts Jack Russell, Dachshund, and unhinged.

When Cora reached out her hands, Libee migrated up her left arm, burrowing between her neck and the long brown curls that spilled over Cora's shoulders. She had wanted to cut her hair short, but her boyfriend informed her girls are prettier with long hair.

Cora didn't know she was meeting her soulmate, or that this warm blur would soften the edges of her structured life spent between classes and her three jobs.

Like many right decisions, it made no logical sense, but it seemed Libee determined on the spot that she must live with Cora. Of course given she was a dog, Libee lacked the capacity to consider that she already had a home with the cop, and Cora was just learning how to make a home for herself. But she was right, and their union would come to pass, overriding logic as good things do. But not yet.

The officer went on to report that he had just gotten Libee from her litter, that she would make a fine pet after he had her long ears and tail cropped.

That night, between the floorboards that separated her bedroom from the officer's kitchen, Cora lay awake, haunted by Libee's abandoned whimpers, howling for what felt like both of their loneliness, both craving forward motion and also rest next to someone warm.

Over the coming days, Cora would offer to walk Libee, the officer would oblige, muttering under bourbon-soaked breath that the dog was terrible on a leash. He was under the assumption that dogs, of course, leash-train themselves, and that obedience was the same as respect.

One day, a couple of weeks before she verbally assaulted the officer, Cora returned home from campus.

"I've had enough of this rat, if you don't take her, I'm giving her to the shelter on Monday," the officer shot out.

Cora lied, mostly to herself. "I'll take her, I'll find her a home."

But she never did look for a home; she knew from their first introduction where the dog would live.

And this is how Cora found herself, two Tuesdays later, in escalating conversation with the cop.

"Of course she shit all over the house!" The heat in Cora's voice brewed like a tea kettle at the base of her lungs. Rising in steam and piercing volume she continued, "You said you would watch her while I took the train to visit my boyfriend in New Jersey, and instead you abandoned her for three days. For three days! She had no food or water or anyone to let her out."

The kettle reached boiling, she slammed the back door.

Cora would soon cut her hair and not the dog's ears. They would drive each other equal parts wild and sane, moving forward together in a glorious blur.

Karlee Fain is an author and founder of Every Body Thrive, an elite coaching practice that shows driven women how to prosper authentically in business and soul in the new economy. She breathes life into her writing with the Powder Keg Writing Workshop run by Suzi Banks Baum.

Visit Karlee's website at: www.everybodythrive.com.

Judith Ralston Ellison

Gotch'a Coming and Going

You know how they do business, those selling risk shields; call it, *in-sure-ants*. Damage occurs: they put it right like it never happened. Yeah sure! Even when you sign all those papers and pay all the money, they fight paying or fixing. Force proof-hoops for you to jump through.

In-sure-ants have all the money and keep the amount a secret. Don't believe me? Try to find out, ask around, research the library. No mystery, why in-sure-ants' office every street corner.

I'm high: mumbling and thinking, paying in-sure-ants premiums with drops of money from an empty pocket.

The little guy, you and me, get on their bus by the law of liability. We ride to the disappointing destination of in-sure-ants paying little or never and blaming you. Scares the pajamas right off you. That's what you were wearing when it happened, right?!

In the car on the road, she, no pajamas but a tank top, not hers, donned in a hurry to go quick to the store. A crash. Dent, glass cracked, phone home.

"Are you alright? Shit what happened? Be right there. Call cops. No wait til I get there." Thinking, you can't keep doing this . . . being scared to live. "Did anyone see you in the dark?"

Drive there but careful in buzzed drink state. Don't need the other dented, smashed. Collision deductible is high. Don't want to spend it this way. Got other things to spend it on like: kids shoes. In headlights looks bad: knocked sign over.

"How fast? Jeez we really didn't need this got so many other things." Lost my job, on unemployment. Small savings in 401k paying for food. "No, I'm not blaming you," but then you turn away and twist mouth in secret. Asking: "Can you drive it home?" Maybe we can fix it without calling the cops." Looking, thinking.

What about the sign: got same paint on it. Town is small. Known who drives what color. Better phone cops or be blamed for leaving scene of accident. "Let me do the talking. No, not going to say was driving."

"Yeah, there was an accident. Hit a road sign out here at the crossroads…" of blame and despair due to not wanting to deal with expensive unexpected events. "We will wait. No hurry. No bodily injury." But it hurts.

"Can you pass the drink test? Breathe deep, try to get the smell gone, walk around, look sober. Why wearing my old big tank top? Everything you got showing."

Damn . . . doesn't look good anyway it's sliced. She has the only paying job, need the money.

"God, what if you don't pass the sober test? Keep breathing, walking, take a mint."

Headlights from town, silent flash. Pulls over.

"Well the car is not too bad, can live with it but the sign . . . thought better call . . . not want any trouble by leaving scene of accident. Jerry off duty? Live couple miles away needed milk from the store for kids' cereal in morning. Yeah, they sell it at the liquor store in the back...nearest to us. Anyway, big store closed. Here's her license insurance registration. Why want mine? Not driving: came after she called. OK...not argue. New co . . . officer, right?"

Think: stand in headlights of his car, stay in the official video. Where is she? God, all will see her hanging out the tank top.

"Cover yourself; OK please." What will our kids say; her judging parents blame you anyway.

Both have to walk toe-to-heel, touch finger to nose, take breath test.

"Blow, blow, blow . . . you're not trying hard enough; better cooperate or else . . . take you in."

Pass, pass. Both just below legal limit.

"Better leave the cars here; will drive you home."

"Thanks officer."

Moves our car straight on the side of road behind the other one. Locks. Hands both sets of keys over.

"Call insurance in the morning. Police report goes automatically to CLUE. They will know, and your premium may go up even if no repairs are done. You will have to pay for the sign damage. Sorry, Jerry would have done same thing."

Quietly shut the rear door of police cruiser after she is out. Sober now. Don't want to talk. Wrap your arms around her for warmth and forgiveness. Should have covered her nakedness earlier.

A 2009 retirement sparked **Judith Ralston Ellison's** imagination for writing. She was awarded a prize for Flash Fiction by Rochester Writers. *Third Wednesday*, published another fiction. *The Detroit Institute of Art's* newsletter published a creative non-fiction essay, and the Michigan State Bar newsletter, *Mentor*, published a fiction story.

Susan Emshwiller
The Wild Grass

I am a retard."

"Don't use that word."

"Retard! Retard! Retard!" She kicks the weathered bench and I'm glad no other families are in the clearing.

"You're not retarded."

"Retard!"

"Please don't use that word. You demean yourself."

She kicks harder. I've got to distract her.

"We should have picnics more often. Isn't it nice and sunny out here?"

"Hot and sunny was the forecast, Mama."

"That's what the weatherman said."

"Hot and sunny all day long. Only not at night when the fireflies are out. They are mean. Always try to burn the house down, down, down to the ground."

She picks a scab on her shin. I want to remind her to

pull her knee socks up so she'll stop scratching those bites, but I don't. My lips press tight to keep from criticizing or controlling. It's so hard not to say anything.

Back of my neck is hot. Did I miss a spot with the sunscreen? Better not have missed on her.

A bee lands and swirls in her lemonade. She's occupied with her scab so I quickly splash the drink to the ground. The creature circles angrily in the wet dirt.

The sandwiches are growing stiff, their edges curling in the sun.

"You wanted a picnic. Aren't you hungry?"

She scrapes at lichen growing on the table. She'll get a splinter under her nail and that'll be the end of the day.

"Are we going to talk about the weather or not?" she asks.

"Yes, the weather. Some of us find it unseasonably warm today."

"And humid like a shower with the fan broken when I disappeared."

She's not forgotten when she couldn't find herself in the mirror.

"But you didn't disappear," I say. The minute it's out I regret it.

She leaps from the picnic table, running across the low mowed circle and into the tall dry grass skirting the woods.

"Come back, there might be snakes," I yell.

She stomps knee-deep among the wildflowers. Pollen and hundreds of little creatures take to the air. Please don't sting her.

"Come back and have a sandwich."

The cicada's high drone is the perfect wrong sound right now. Can't they stop for five minutes? Can't everything stop for five minutes?

"We can take off the relish if it's not a relish day."

"Will the snakes bite if I step on them?"

"Please help me eat these, darling."

She turns to me, standing stiffly, legs hidden by the yellow weeds. "Who are you calling darling?" she asks.

"You're darling, sweetheart."

She takes a step backward. There must be a slope because the weeds reach her waist now. Why did we come here? We should have stayed home. We could have had a picnic in the backyard.

"Which is it? Darling or Sweetheart?" she asks, a challenge in her voice.

What is the right answer? What will bring her out of the wild grass?

She takes another step back. She's up to her shoulders, only a few yards from the darkness of the pines and who knows what's in there.

Don't let her see my panic. "Which do you prefer?" I ask, spreading a smile.

"I prefer. I prefer. When did I get that option?"

The sun on my neck is definitely burning. No matter how hard I try, there's always a place I miss and there's always pain because of it.

She takes another step toward the forest darkness, a disembodied head hovering over the dense field. Fear rises in my throat. This is a taste of what's to come.

"It's your choice. Darling—Sweetheart. Which do you prefer?"

"I prefer Retard, Mama. Call me Retard."

Susan Emshwiller is a produced screenwriter (co-writer of the film "Pollock"), filmmaker, published playwright and short story writer. Recent or upcoming publications include *The Magazine of Fantasy and Science Fiction, Dramatists Play Service, Independent Ink, Gone Lawn,* and *Black Heart Magazine.* She teaches screenwriting at North Carolina State University. Visit Susan at www.susanemshwiller.com.

Judy Burke
Finding Things

I won't sit in the red chair anymore. It used to be my throne in the kitchen, the most comfortable spot—tucked between the counter with the big-leafed plant and the bay windows, facing the backyard. It was separate from the working part of the kitchen: the sink and stove, the "sit-down" counter; although you could hear everything, and see, too, if you sat forward a bit and peeped over the countertop between the leaves.

I'd sit curled up in the red over-stuffed club chair and watch the birds at the feeder outside the window while I drank my tea. I was in the kitchen, but not visible, though they all knew where to find me. The red chair was a protected cove I could sail into when I'd get caught up in the slipstream of kindergarten woes and middle-school anxieties; of angst over boys or upsets in class, of fibs uncovered and daily betrayals, of being kicked in the nuts by a best friend, of squabbles, of their worries, all of which so easily became mine.

I'd sit in the red chair and look at the birds—sparrows, mostly; a cardinal couple, chickadees, a family of goldfinches much like mine, and a pileated woodpecker. They'd fly between the feeder on the trellis and the big beech tree with the broken rope ladder, and back again over the yard littered with homemade wooden swords and shields, dress up clothes, World War II dug-outs, hula hoops, dinosaur figures, My Little Ponies and water pistols, depending on who had played what last.

In the summer the windows would be open, and the trellis would be covered with morning glories in the daylight and moonflowers at night. The rhythmic sounds of all-day play would ease into the creak of crickets and tree frogs, all of it drowning out the air-conditioner next door. In the winter, the cold glass panes and bleakness of the yard would settle me deeper in the cushions, and I would watch the snow mount and look for who came home first and see what their day was like by how they walked from the car or the school bus and climbed the steps to the back door.

Sometimes, depending less on their size than on the quality of their day, they'd head right to my lap and settle there for a spell, telling me their deepest troubles and hopes. The privacy of the chair gave them license to share secrets, and I'd listen and nod, trusted and privileged. I'd be there when math overwhelmed, when friendships took a dangerous turn, and always when something couldn't be found. I'd be there to dry tears, scratch backs, marvel. Sometimes I sat in disapproval and wasn't approached at all.

Lately, my time in the chair has been troubling. The current of small troubles that used to overwhelm is dealt with out of my sphere, and the kitchen is often empty. When I sit there to watch the birds, it's without that sense of refuge. Instead of settling into a certain kind of peace, I find I'm at loose ends, and brooding. When I sit in the chair now, unless I'm very tired, or putting on my shoes, I feel the silence and the empty room.

I just won't sit there anymore. Activity suits me these days. I'm in the yard where children used to be, digging and pruning away. Or I'll go to the writing desk in the sun porch. There's a nice view into the side yard and the neighbor's garden and the street beyond. I like the quiet there, the different perspective; and I've also come to like the distant and occasional sound of people in the kitchen, finding things on their own.

Judy Burke lived and worked in New York as an actress for the past 35 years, and has recently moved back to her hometown of Norfolk, VA. She finds the slower pace is improving her disposition.

Alyssa N. Vaughn
Reactions

Mrs. Delaney seemed incapable of calming herself; she had been crying hysterically for nearly two and a half hours. Joanie, the head nurse on duty in that wing, was beginning to suspect that she'd soon have to fetch an IV for Mrs. Delaney to keep her from dehydrating. The detective was displaying saint-like patience as he attempted to record her statement. His partner had expertly extricated herself to interview Mr. Jason Delaney, Mrs. Delaney's son, and his wife Mrs. Valerie Ingersoll. It was their son who was in the pediatric ward, having suffered severe anaphylactic shock after ingesting strawberries.

Joanie had been the one to call in the police after Mrs. Delaney, her son and daughter-in-law began shouting at each other across the child's hospital bed. She hadn't caught it all, but she had heard enough to make it clear that the boy hadn't eaten the strawberries by accident; someone had either been negligent in monitoring the child or he had been given the food deliberately.

After the statements had been taken, Mrs. Delaney was bundled into a cab and sent home, protesting the entire time that she needed to be with her grandson. Mr. Delaney went off to obtain some dinner for himself and his wife, and Mrs. Ingersoll, absolutely exhausted, sat at her son's bedside. The detectives met Joanie in the staff breakroom.

"What do you think?" asked Joanie, pouring them all fresh cups of coffee.

Detective Yu, who had spent the last four hours with the distraught grandmother, sighed heavily.

"It's nearly impossible to say. They just seem to be throwing wild accusations at each other. Maybe it's a simple case of bad blood and picking a sad opportunity to bring it to light."

His partner, Detective Rubio, shook her head.

"No way, it was definitely the mother-in-law. That lady's got a screw loose."

Joanie motioned them to sit at a table. "Tell me what you can," she said.

Detective Rubio began.

"The allergy is well established in the family. The boy's maternal aunt and grandmother have had it. So they watched for it, even before he was officially diagnosed. They didn't keep any strawberries in the house and they never used them in any recipes. Today was the kid's fourth birthday and most of the family was over for a party. At no point in the day was the kid ever out of the parents' sight."

"Never?" asked Joanie.

"Well, not until after cake when mom went to the bathroom and dad went out in the front yard to say goodbye to his grandparents. When he came back inside, the dad said his mother was bent over the kid who was going into shock."

Rubio shrugged.

"The only problem is, they can't prove she gave him anything; there weren't any incriminating wrappers or bottles in the trash, so they have no idea what he actually ate."

"The old lady kept insisting that there must have been some traces on one of the dishes the relatives brought," Yu interjected. "It was a potluck, and she said that her daughter-in-law is only blaming her because of some kind of grudge."

Joanie nodded thoughtfully, and took a long sip from her coffee.

"I think," she said slowly, "that you ought to check that big white handbag the grandma was clinging to earlier today."

"I dunno" said Yu doubtfully. "If she had stashed something in there, wouldn't she have ditched it by now?"

"She'd find it difficult," said Joanie unblushingly, "since it's hidden behind the counter in the nurses' station."

The detectives stared at her for a moment, then Yu took off, jogging down the hallway to grab the bag. Rubio grinned at Joanie.

"She left it in the ladies' room," Joanie said levelly. "Perfectly legal."

"I forgot," said Rubio with a twinkle, "that you had a mother-in-law like that, too."

"Living with crazy that long," Joanie sighed, "teaches you to recognize it pretty quickly. More coffee?"

"Absolutely."

Alyssa N Vaughn is an author and reviewer from Dallas, Texas, where she lives with her husband, 8-month-old son, and two dogs. Her grandfather got young Alyssa hooked on Agatha Christie, and recently she got herself hooked on a certain Mother-In-Law themed subreddit. *Reactions* is her tribute to both.

Andrew Gottlieb
Morale Event

That Saturday, he walked all over the city, buying signs from homeless people. He knew many of them, and it was good exercise: to really get good signs, he had to cover some territory. There was never a density; too many signs in one place wasn't a useful strategy. People with money stopped giving if confronted with too much need. It was an artform really, getting people to part with money.

Most of the signs were on cardboard, with uneven edges and large, block letters in black ink. Some had a bend that made them flappy. They said a variety of things like: ANYTHING HELPS JUST TRYING TO SURVIVE GOD BLESS; or HARD TIMES 3 KIDS PLEASE HELP; or WILL WORK FOR FOOD I'M LIKE YOU HELP ME PLEASE.

He offered five dollars for each sign, but allowed himself to be negotiated up to ten.

He could carry around a few, but cardboard got bulky so then he stacked them in his car, some in his back seat, the rest in the trunk. He waved to people who knew him.

He stopped for lunch, eating half an Italian sub, later trading the other half for a sign on the back of an old pizza box.

Monday, in the third-floor conference room at the corporation where he worked, ahead of the big monthly marketing meeting, he stacked the signs on the table. He had borrowed a cart from the mail room to get the signs upstairs. A few minutes ahead of the meeting, employees started strolling in with their coffee and laptops. They looked over the signs with amusement. He told them there was one for everyone and to take the sign that spoke to them the most.

They all laughed and said he was very creative. Everyone wanted a sign that said some form of HELP ME on it, but some had to settle for ANYTHING HELPS signs. By the afternoon, the signs were all over the office, propped against cubicle walls or leaning in office windows. There was chuckling, and it brightened everyone's day. The Operations Program Manager's sign said, I WON'T LIE I NEED A BEER. The clerk's sign said, JUST TRYING TO GET BY. There was sign-swapping and jealousies over the good ones.

Later, he went from office to office. The conversations were never long. He collected a lot of money per sign. The admin opened her purse and gave him $100, just like that. The VP wasn't as generous. By the end of the day, he'd made money on every single sign.

The next day, at the homeless shelter, he donated almost all of it, but held back some, planning his next trip out to buy more signs. He was part of a project team with Finance, and they had a monthly meeting coming up. The Finance guys made bank. He'd enjoy this one even more.

He could walk the city this weekend. He'd start at five again, but would go up to ten, if needed.

Andrew C. Gottlieb lives and writes in Irvine, California. His work has appeared in *American Fiction, Best New Poets, Denver Quarterly, Ecotone, The Fly Fish Journal, Mississippi Review, Orion,* and *Poetry Northwest*. His new poetry chapbook, *Flow Variations,* is published by Finishing Line Press (December 2017).

Say hello at: www.andrewcgottlieb.com.

Caren Stuart
At the Crossroads

Umberto sits in the patch of grass under the pink mimosa tree at the edge of the gravel lot of Elois' Country Diner at the crossroads of Loop Road and Old NC 29. He savors the last drop of black coffee in his large To-Go cup, rises slowly, and grimaces as he straightens his right leg. He whispers his short prayer of thanks for his shrapnel. Lots of guys weren't as lucky as he'd been.

It's Wednesday morning. Umberto has delivered a bucket of mixed salad greens, large yellow onions, and green peppers from his farm for Elois to work into her lunch menu. Three times each week he walks the better part of a mile to bring her fresh produce from his roadside Pay-What-You-Can stand. It's a nice walk, good for his body, and a good deed for his soul, this donation of his bounty, his secret penance for the thousands of gallons of poison he'd rained down on the farmlands of 'Nam in '71.

He's eaten today's egg and cheese butter biscuit, dropped his vegetables off here, and had a good morning coffee, so he wraps his thin green plaid work shirt around his head for protection from a sun that bakes hot during his slow walks back home. A white haired couple in church clothes is leaving the diner, making their way across the lot toward a shiny, older model blue Buick. Umberto sees that a back tire is dangerously low and is able to catch the man's eye for an instant, but not long enough to motion toward the tire. The man has looked away from Umberto, hooked an arm into his wife's arm, and quickened their pace toward their car.

Umberto limps as fast as he's able toward the couple, says, "Excuse me," just loudly enough to draw attention to his finger pointing out their bad tire. But the couple gets into their car without looking at Umberto, his finger, or their tire. They get in, lock their doors, buckle up.

Umberto reaches the car as the engine turns over, tap taps the wife's window with his empty paper cup, and motions with his free hand to please roll down the window. The window motor grumbles but the window shuts tighter. Umberto tap taps and motions again. The window hisses down an inch or so and stops. Then it drops a few inches, drops down two or three more, then grinds up a few inches, down a few, up again. And it stops. Opens three or four inches. Enough to speak through. But before Umberto can warn the couple about their tire, the man leans across his wife, looks up sternly at Umberto, commands, "Don't buy liquor or drugs with this money!" and the wife pokes a handful of coins through the window just before its groaning motor has sealed it closed once again.

Now the car engine roars fiercely and Umberto startles backward. He straightens as the transmission slams hard into gear. The shiny blue Buick fast jabs into reverse. Lunges up into drive. Belches gravel and growls as it swerves out of the lot and out onto Old NC 29.

"Looks like someone's in a hurry to get somewhere." Genevieve calls loudly, tilting her head toward the vanishing car, shifting textbooks on her arm as the diner door shuts behind her.

Umberto nods. "A rush to judgment," he answers, placing his curious cup of change into Genevieve's free hand. "Your tip of the day, Miss," he adds. And he smiles. At the pink mimosa tree. He heads home.

Caren Stuart lives joyfully in the wilds of Chatham County, NC (with her husband, a dog, and a cat) where she writes poetry and fiction and creates and sells her "convoluted notions" jewelry, art, and crafts. Her award-winning poetry's been widely published. This is the first publication of her fiction.

Visit her website: www.facebook.com/convolutednotions.

Joy Ross Davis
Silver Sequins

Jeanie Martin stood outside the huge display window at Harrod's Boutique, her eyes fixed on a sequined sweater the color of the sea. Only an hour before, her husband had said, "C'mon. Let's go to the mall."

"But I'm not dressed for it," she'd replied, glancing down at her baggy brown sweat pants and yellow oversized tee shirt. "Can you give me a few minutes to change?"

And he, dressed in a fine Italian three-piece suit, white dress shirt, and striped tie, grabbed the keys off the hook.

"Let's go," he said. "Now. We'll stop at Ruby Tuesdays on the way back. The fridge is about empty and there doesn't seem to be anything cooking on the stove."

Jeanie grabbed her purse, smoothed on some lip gloss, ran her fingers through her just-washed hair, and followed him.

He said he had business to attend to at The Pistol Parlor, private client-attorney business, the kind she was never allowed to witness. He handed her two slim stacks of bills, both secured by wide rubber bands.

"Ten one-hundred-dollar bills," he said. "Go next door to the boutique and buy whatever you want, but use good taste. You need an outfit for the shindig at The Relay House next week. Something dressy. I'll check on you when I finish."

"And you want me to pick it out myself?" Jeanie asked. "You hardly ever let me pick out my own clothes."

He chuckled. "Well, Sugar, that's because you don't have very good taste. But give it a try. Maybe my sense of style has rubbed off on you in the four years we've been married. Pick out what you want at Harrod's, but I have the final say."

And with that, he walked away.

And now, she was here, gazing at the beautiful sea-blue sweater. The silver sequins trailed down the long sleeves and around the neckline, and as the sweater turned on its pedestal, it shimmered.

Jeanie peeked around the corner to see if the store was crowded, and seeing no one else inside but the clerk, she walked in, her steps soft so as not to attract attention. But a bell rang as she entered, and the clerk came to her immediately. He eyed her up and down, a look of utter disgust on his face.

Jeanie smoothed her tee shirt, adjusted her purse, and turned toward the sweater to hide the flush that came to her cheeks.

"May I help you?" the clerk asked and startled her. He was a tall man dressed in a suit and tie, his hands clasped at his waist.

"I...I like this sweater in the window," Jeanie said and pointed. "This one."

The clerk raised an eyebrow. "Oh, but that sweater is very expensive." He dismissed her with a wave of his hand. "I'm afraid that we have very little that would suit you. Perhaps another place would be a better choice."

"But I'd like to see the sweater," Jeanie said.

"I'm sorry, but it wouldn't fit you," the clerk said.

Jeanie lowered her head and walked away. She heard the bell ding as she stepped out of the store, just in time to see her husband coming toward her, a big smile on his handsome face.

"Well, Sugar, what did you buy?"

Jeanie pointed to the sweater in the window. "I...I wanted that sweater, but the clerk said I should try another store."

She saw the look, then, that look he got when his temper was about to explode. "No, Anthony, please,

please don't do anything."

Her heart pounded as she watched the clerk bag up something and hand it to her husband.

And she watched as that same clerk's face blanched pure white when Anthony put his business card on the counter, then leaned in and whispered something to him.

The clerk put his hands to his mouth.

"How does it feel to have made your very last sale?" Anthony said and laughed. "See you in court."

Two years later, the sweater lies still folded in the bureau drawer in the new apartment, never once worn. Jeanie hardly thinks of it anymore, never sees Anthony, and takes pride in the new job as the Executive Secretary of his biggest rival.

Occasionally, when the drawer is opened, light plays on the sweater's silver sequins and casts a warm glow all around. She smiles and moves on.

Joy Ross Davis is a student of the romance, lore, and magic of the black hills of Tennessee. She lives in Alabama with her son and three rescue dogs and writes imaginative fiction.

Find her on Facebook at: www.facebook.com/jdavisangelwriter.

Judy Burke
Balloon

When the white balloon escaped the little girl's grasp and began a slow ascent towards the vaulted roof of Grand Central Terminal, her initial reaction was dismay, and a cry of distress. It was a particularly large balloon that seemed to glow, whitish silver, and she had received it when her mother had bought her a pair of black and white saddle shoes at the Stride Rite Shoe Store on 34th Street. All through the eight-block walk up Lexington Avenue toward the train station, she had held the balloon tight, especially when the wind fought her for it, and it occasionally bumped against a grown-up hurrying past.

"Hold tight!" her mother said repeatedly, and wanted to tie it to the little girl's wrist so she wouldn't lose it, but the little girl wouldn't allow it. She liked the feel of the ribbon in her hand. She liked the tug of the balloon, and the satisfaction of keeping it safe, minding its progress toward the station and the train home. She thought of how nice the ride home would be, looking out the window of the train, her face in the glass with the balloon by her side, reflected as well. But in the heat and confusion of the station, as she struggled to unbutton the top button of her sweater, the balloon made its escape.

"Ohh!" she cried, and by the time her mother turned to look the balloon was beyond reach, though she continued to hold out her hand for it, as if it might come back.

Her mother put her packages down and picked the little girl up. The two of them watched as the balloon slowly rose, stoically, majestically towards the far away ceiling of Grand Central, which was stenciled with outlines of all the constellations in the heavens. As it rose, the height of the ceiling became apparent. It climbed up and up, as if drawn; and as it did, the ceiling seemed to recede farther and farther away.

Other passengers hurrying to catch their trains noticed the beautiful silver white flight of the balloon as it ascended, and they also stopped to watch, necks craning in the Concourse, wondering how long it would take to make it to the top, and oh, how beautiful it was on its journey. For a minute, almost everyone who had been rushing, to trains, or home, or work or shopping or shows, stopped, pointing up at the little girl's balloon, smiling as it moved away from them up towards the stars.

The little girl held her mother's hand all the way to the train. She missed the feel of the ribbon and thought she might cry for the loss of the balloon, but she didn't. As the train headed home and she looked out the window at her small face reflected, and the river beyond, she felt proud of how pretty it had been, rising so bravely on its way to disappearing; and of how everyone in the station came to love it, and watch it on its way.

Judy Burke lived and worked in New York as an actress for the past 35 years, and has recently moved back to her hometown of Norfolk, VA. She finds the slower pace is improving her disposition.

"Books are the plane,
and the train, and the road.
They are the destination,
and the journey.
They are home."
—Anna Quindlen

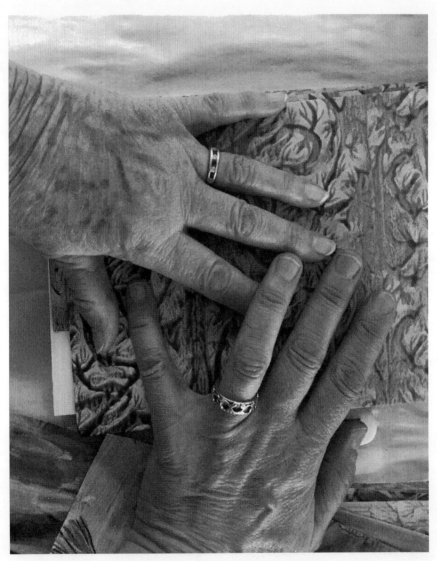

Matching Rings © Suzi Banks Baum

Elizabeth Burton
An Unlikely Friend

*E*dith was disappointed when Tiffany Berry moved in across the street. She had hoped someone her own age would buy the house with the inviting front porch. She'd imagined lazy mornings spent on that porch having coffee and chatting with her new friend about their cats as they waved to neighbors going about their day. So, the presence of young Tiffany Berry, with her shocking pink hair and Buster, the giant white dog that bounded around the house and yard as if he were going back and forth to a fire, dismayed Edith.

A certain level of dismay had been her constant companion since Larry passed away a year ago. Things which had been commonplace, even small things, such as servicing the car, were now frighteningly unfamiliar without Larry to do them with her. Edith had looked forward to the distraction of someone new in her life.

But Tiffany was not what she'd been looking for.

Oh, she had to admit the girl (she couldn't think of anyone with pink hair as a woman) was friendly. Instead of waiting for Edith and all the other neighbors to welcome her to the neighborhood, she'd brought over small containers of homemade cocoa wrapped in decorative yellow bows. Edith had been gracious, inviting the girl and her dog into the living room, even as her cat's eyes widened. She hadn't complained when she'd had to sweep up dog hair for two days afterward. It's just that she longed for the kind of deeper companionship only a true friend could provide. And a friend who was a neighbor would have been perfect.

One day, about a month after Tiffany moved in, Edith was in her front yard pulling up weeds. Suddenly, she felt out of breath. The house and the cell phone she'd left inside seemed very far away. A strange, electric feeling started moving up her spine into her neck and jaw. When the electric feeling turned into pain, she knew something was very wrong. She tried to get up, but the yard and the sky began spinning. She could hear someone calling her name, but she couldn't respond. She heard the voice call out, "Buster, stay!" and as she began shivering, she felt the dog's warm body lie down carefully against her.

When she woke up, it took her a few minutes to realize she was in a hospital. Her mind and body seemed to be separate from each other: her mind was alert and clear; her body sluggish. She had to blink a few times before the room came into focus. Gingerly, she turned her head, drawing the attention of a nurse walking by.

"Your friend will be glad to know you're awake," she said. "She's been here ever since you were brought in."

Friend? Edith wondered. She tried to say something, but her mouth was so dry the words wouldn't come out.

The nurse disappeared and in a few seconds, Tiffany walked in. "How are you feeling?"

Edith opened her mouth but shook her head. Understanding the problem, Tiffany reached for a cup of water beside the bed and offered the straw to her. Edith drank long and slow, the water feeling like a renewal.

"What happened?" she finally croaked.

"You had a heart attack," Tiffany said. "But thankfully, I saw the whole thing and called for help. You're going to be fine."

Tiffany came to visit every day Edith was in the hospital. She brought romance novels, the kind Edith had been too embarrassed to read when Larry was alive, and the two women laughed over them until they cried. Edith learned that Buster and her cat had formed an alliance, and that her flowers were blooming.

"We're all excited to have you back home," Tiffany confided. "It's been lonely without you there."

Over the next few weeks, Edith and Tiffany became closer. Edith found out that Tiffany's own husband had died in a car accident and Buster was all she had in the world. She'd moved to town to make a new start. She was an illustrator of greeting cards, so she worked from home.

Edith felt comfortable in the young woman's presence, and it wasn't too long before the two were going in and out of each other's houses as easily as her own. That coffee Edith had been looking forward to? They had it each morning on Tiffany's porch, surrounded by Buster and his new friend, Edith's cat.

Elizabeth Burton lives in Central Kentucky with her husband and two willful dogs. She holds an MFA and her stories have appeared in several anthologies, as well as *Roanoke Review, Waypoints, The Grief Diaries, Kentucky Review, Chautauqua,* and forthcoming in *The Louisville Review* and *The MacGuffin.*

Learn more at: elizabethburtonwriter.com.

Leigh Fisher
Ironic Spells

He drummed his fingers against the metal tray and for once, he was rather glad that prison food was completely terrible. Being served an uncooked potato, onion, and a piece of bread made for a disgusting meal; but the ingredients were good for beginning an enchantment. The guards removed every type of artifact that they thought could allow him to cast a spell, but they hadn't anticipated that something as insignificant as an onion could help him.

"Miss Harriet, I need you to do one favor for me," he said as he leaned against the wall that connected to her cell.

"Why should I help a man who hasn't even told me his name?"

"We've both been imprisoned by the town guard and we want to get out. I'd say that gives us so much more in common than most people who decide to share drinks."

He could hear her scoff and with the way it echoed, he was fairly certain any other prisoners further down in the cell block could hear her as well. Being trapped in a dungeon beneath the city most certainly had *not* been on his to-do list for that week. The building was rather new, and the cells weren't that dirty, but they still had the traditional cold, stone walls and a poor excuse for a cot that was scarcely more than a blanket on the floor.

"Sounds like you'll get a drink with anyone wearing a skirt," she said disapprovingly.

"Au contraire, I know several male mages who wear garments similar to skirts, and I personally would not get drinks with them for love or money."

"You're too cheerful for someone in prison."

He grabbed the onion off the tray and tossed it up and down. "You've got a carrot, right?"

"And bread, but there's a moldy spot on it."

He blinked in surprise. "Really? Mold? That's even better."

"There's something *really* wrong with you."

"Can I have the bread?"

"Why?" she asked, her voice taking on an edge of skepticism.

"For a little magic trick," he said, trying to sound as innocent as possible.

"On the off chance it works, there'll be something in it

for me since I helped?"

His lips curled into a smile. "Of course."

She tossed the roll out onto the floor between their cells. The moment he saw it tumble onto the floor, he dropped to his knees and pounced on it like a cat on a mouse. He pulled it inside his cell and hurriedly knelt down in front of the lock.

He traced his finger in a circle around the moldy spot on the bread, channeling the different types of energy in the bacteria growing on it. He placed it on the floor parallel to the lock and then reached for the onion, ripping off its outer layer. When he opened his eyes again, the mold on the bread was growing a hundred times faster than ordinary mold would, quickly engulfing the entire roll.

He placed the onion beside it and watched as the extremely rudimentary enchantment blossomed. It was just a few seconds before the onion disappeared and the moldy mass started to move.

"Whatever you're doing over there, it smells horrible," Harriet said in disgust.

"It's the sweet smell of freedom."

As he spoke, the mold creature started to slide up the bars toward the lock. It pushed itself inside the keyhole and filled up the space between the tumblers until he heard a metallic popping sound. It was all he could do to keep from laughing as the lock released and he pushed the door open.

"Holy hell, it worked," she said.

A look of shock registered on her surprisingly youthful face. For how terse her voice sounded, he hadn't been expecting such a young woman.

"Indeed, I'm quite the mage."

He started to walk over to the door when she yelled for him.

"Wait! Don't forget our agreement."

"It'd take quite a while for me to find the key for your cell."

"Do not leave me," she said, jumping to her feet as she grabbed the bars of her cell and shook them.

"Sorry, honey," he said with a shrug, "I forgot to mention it, but lying is why I was thrown in here."

Leigh Fisher is from New Jersey, works in an office, and is a writer around the clock. She is an historical fiction enthusiast, with an avid interest in Chinese history. She has been published in *Five 2 One Magazine*, *The Missing Slate*, *Heater Magazine*, and *Referential Magazine*.

Learn more at: www.LeighFisher.org.

"Books are a uniquely portable magic."

—Stephen King

Birds in Snowy Trees © Anne Anthony

Angela Kubinec
Snow Swept

*I*ce cracks beneath our boots as we make our way from the plaza to the museum. Chunks of it climb from the sidewalk, graze our shins and kiss our collars. Inside, the elevator rises and opens and from the galleries, visitors race us to the balcony where the snow soars from the ground, drifts unassembling, falling up and dispersing so widely that it looks like stars.

The earlier rain now washing the snow. The trees regaining their leaves, looping onto branches from the low side up. Roots tiptoeing out of the ground, setting themselves free, looking more and more like tangled hair, drifting toward an unknown sky. Confused weeds, walls of hedges, grass both green and yellow, bouquets unblooming while joining in.

Roofs and furniture rising as if tethered to balloons, all of them rectangular from below. Like blocks picked up by an unseen toddler. No attic waiting for a purge. Decorative items floating together, upsetting the décor of the heavens. Nothing tumbling, nothing colliding, no arguing over importance. No clamoring for space. High

School annuals now as equally unmoored as first edition copies of *The Grapes of Wrath*. Carpets coming unglued as if trained by Aladdin. Doors impossible to determine whether open or closed. Pebbles and rocks softly clicking, growing into piles, approaching the exosphere backward from their point of rest. Stalagmites and stalactites maintaining their relationship, while we remain confused about which is which.

Cars resembling tragic accidents without the dents or blood. Lawn mowers and weed trimmers at last relaxed. All the groceries looking the same, just on ever higher shelves, with the words on their labels made hieroglyphic. Streetlights becoming distant lollipops. Laundry, both wet and dry, covering the space above like Flags of the World. Lamps, hairdryers, blenders, washing machines, computers, stoves, televisions, all stringing black tails behind them, forever unplugged. Cosmetic confetti leaving makeup bags of startled painted faces.

Money, all the money, the coins, the checkbooks and credit cards, children's piggy banks, becoming ever less important. Identification made pointless. Modes of delineation, posts, barbed wire, chain link fences, iron gates, each one threating to pierce it all. The streets, roads, and bridges peeling themselves away in unison, making a net that catches nothing. Knitting needles like arrows, balls of yarn unwinding. Showers and faucets dripping in the wrong direction, quietly awaiting their turn to be loosened from their joints. Flags of the World reassembling themselves in the stripe of the United Nations. Bottoms of soda bottles making irregular polka dots among it all.

Tears wetting bangs.

The contents of every open drawer, no matter how mundane or shameful, slipping above. Forks, panties, pizza cutters, envelopes, pencils, lost scissors, lubricants. Trashcans hugging their lids. But still, the litter, the litter, the litter. Boats never sinking. Boats that did sink, being revived. Rods, reels, fishing lines, bobbers and sinkers, all looking for life that is not there. Sneezing and coughing becoming less an issue of manners. Other traditionally downward functions turning themselves into nightmares. Drug addicts and alcoholics grabbing and crying, the things they need being removed from their hands. Sliding from mothers' grasps are pacifiers, baby bottles, both clean and dirty diapers—each flecking the clouds with bits of blue, pink, and white. Sprinkles of powder. Everyone's engagement ring making unreachable sparkles. Topaz, ruby, sapphire, garnet, gold, silver, platinum, titanium, every metal known. Multitudinous faces in family photos, introducing themselves as if heading toward a holiday dinner.

Flies no longer flying.

The water ascending, holding sharks and jellyfish and creatures that crawl, towering underneath, leaving us to look in wonder at the space of things that are not.

Angela Kubinec is a Senior Editor at Easy Street Magazine. Her story, *23 Images in Your Gallery of Absent Things*, received an honorable mention in the 2017 Glimmer Train Fall Fiction Open, and was also named finalist in the Black Warrior Review 2017 Contest in Poetry, Fiction and Nonfiction.

Debbie Voisey
Spark

The hand touch was like an explosion. Just like that: BOOM! Soft skin against rough callous. He had pink scrubbed skin with tiny spider veins of indelible black. He looked like he knew his way around a car engine. They had met on a blind date at her best friend Anne's house. Although, not technically a blind date because she knew him, from afar. He'd lived in the same neighbourhood as her practically all their lives. Anne said that he had wanted to go out with her for ages.

"Oh sorry, after you." Matt's face now going as pink as his Swarfega scrubbed hands, his ears glowing. He pushed the sugar towards her. Paula thought that he looked like he was going to throw up.

They were sitting in a coffee shop in town, the one whose window faced down the high street. She said she loved to watch people with their mysterious shopping bags; liked to imagine what was inside.

She drank two flat whites. Her addiction, she said.

Matt watched her face as she looked out of the window, drinking in those shopping bags along with her coffee. He thought that she was like a child who had not had much in her life. Or maybe one who had seen way more than she should and wanted things to finally be simple. To just come down to what was in your bags.

They talked about work a little. She said she wished she had followed her heart and her dream of becoming a nurse, but that 'life got in the way.' He asked how, and her answer floored him.

"You have to heal yourself before you have the right to try and heal anyone else."

He wanted to ask more, but his shortness of breath stopped him. He wondered what had hurt her so badly that she could not heal. He tried to think back to when they were kids and he would watch her playing in the street with her younger sister, who she protected fiercely. If anyone messed with her then they had Paula to answer to. So, he knew that she could heal others; it was apparently just herself she had trouble with.

Around them the noises of a match day Saturday; the street thronged with pint drinkers, a frantic sort of white noise in the air. In the café, fresh spring air wafted in from the street, bright with promise and heavy with hope.

Paula was beautiful, Matt thought. He found his breath quickening, his palms slick. Fifteen years. Fifteen years he had watched her; with this boy or that, this man then that. Stood on the side lines, like a football manager. Like his beloved team's manager.

Paula nodded her head towards the window. Towards the men and women, kids and friends. Giddy in their blue tops and scarves, moving like a sea towards the football ground.

"Are you sure you don't want to go to the match?" she asked.

Semi-final day, on the most beautiful of days, the sky as pale blue as the football supporters' clothes. His team had made it, for the first time, by the skin of their teeth.

Some things you wait for all your life and when they happen, when they finally happen, you don't ever want to let go.

"I'm happy here," he said, and outside, the crowd-ocean flowed on.

Debbi Voisey lives in Stoke-on-Trent in the United Kingdom. Her stories appear in print anthologies—*Bath Short Story Award 2015, National Flash Fiction Day 2016* and *Ellipsis: One*—and online at *Storgy, Litro, Ad Hoc, Paragraph Planet, National Flash Flood 2017* and *Ellipsis Zine*.

Learn more at: debbivoisey.co.uk

Charlotte Byrne
Monday Morning

The juices are always the worst part of the job. It's never so bad when it rains, and they all get washed away. But on hot days like today, the juices can make the difference as to whether it's a good day or a bad one.

I grab the two black sacks nearest to me on the kerb and launch them into the compacter. It's then that I face the full might of the juices as one of the sacks gets stuck. It bursts, showering me with grease and grime and whatever else number 47 has thrown out.

"Damn!" I wipe my face with the crease of my elbow because my gloves are smothered in everything. When I inspect it, there's remnants of vegetables mixed in with gravy and tiny chicken bones, and I wonder the foxes haven't had it out overnight. I try and shake off the Sunday dinner when Raj calls to me.

"Dan, over here!"

I throw on the last two sacks, ducking as they fall just in case, and head to Raj's side of the street. I don't look for traffic because it's still too early. It's dark, but I can see his Cheshire Cat teeth as I jog towards him.

"Won't it do for your boy?"

I squint at what he's got in his hands. Jackpot! Somebody has cleared out their garage and it's time for us to pick up our perks. I've had all sorts over the years, ornaments and electricals from the year zero that I either palm off as vintage or keep for the house. The best find was an old radiogram that I managed to restore; it still plays all the LPs Shel and I collected when we were courting. But it's nothing compared to what Raj has picked up and I feel my dinner-smeared cheeks break into a grin to match his.

It's a rusty Raleigh Chopper. One of the wheels is missing. It's caked in bird shit and the paintwork has seen better days, but it's definitely a C-H-O-P-P-E-R. You can still see the letters on the down tube, even in the monochrome of the early morning.

"Can I have it?" My throat sticks. Sam has been wanting a bike for ages.

Raj tuts and thrusts it at me, shooting me a look that tells me not to ask silly questions. I tell him thanks and jog up to the cab of the truck, throwing it in next to Gary who looks bored as arseholes in the driver's seat. He glances at my treasure and spits out of the window.

"More junk?"

I let it fly over my head and head back to my patch. The people at 49 have had a party. The sacks are overflowing and there are beer cans and crisp packets on the pavement. I'm not picking them up. I heave the open sacks up into the compacter.

I try and shift one of the tied sacks quickly, but it has been overstuffed and splits up the side. More beer cans and a few jars fall out. And a used sanitary towel. Ugh. All rubbish reeks, but you do get used to it. There's just something about jam rags that makes me want to throw up. I screw my face up as I chuck it in the compacter, and I think of Shel when she used to flush them down the toilet. I'd told her it was a job for the bin men, never thinking that one day I'd be doing it myself.

I pick up the box at number 51. I don't miss her, but I can't wait for her to bring Sam around next Saturday. It's my day to have him and I'll have the bike all done up for him, and I'll have a good scrub for the occasion.

I throw the box in and realise I've got sick on my gloves.

Charlotte Byrne graduated with an MA in Creative Writing in 2016. Her short story, *Soldiers All*, can be found in *Tales of the World* (2013, DualBooks), and her two pieces, *Sardines,* and *Not Tonight*, are published in *Purple Lights* (2016, Fincham Press). When not writing, she mothers dogs.

"Stories make us
more alive, more human,
more courageous,
more loving."
— Madeleine L'Engle

Many Hearts © Suzi Banks Baum

Heidi Espenscheid Nibbelink
Love Test

I've had a cold since Thursday and I literally can't live without a cough drop inside my mouth every single minute. I eat with one in, I drink tea with one in, I even sleep with one in, although I worry about choking and dying, and pray that when I suck it down my windpipe it will be sufficiently small and thin so that it will dissolve in time for me to start breathing again so I can survive with only minimal brain damage and go on to lead a fulfilling life. If I could be certain that an episode of oxygen deprivation would turn down the lights on the anxiety center, the depression generator, the impaired executive-functioning switchboard, I'd climb aboard that train and ride it all the way to Grand Central Station.

When I'm sick, my sweet roommate Kiki brings me magazines and Cup O' Noodles. She's an actress who is always going on auditions, so she's terrified of catching anything. She sets my food on the carpet outside my bedroom door and taps lightly four times. I have to count to ten before I open the door to give her time to get out of germ range.

"Thanks!" I text her, or "Chicken flavor again?" or "Jennifer Chastain did NOT wear it better." I am sick often. I have taken measures to ensure I never run out of cough drops.

When I'm not sick, Kiki and I sit on our tiny third-floor balcony and blow soap bubbles across the alley, trying to get them to float as far as the neighboring rooftop. There are kids' toys strewn around that building's entrance. I like to think of children looking up at us from their bedroom windows, jealous of us grown-ups who can sit on the balcony and drink Mike's Hard Lemonade and hold bubble contests while they have to finish their homework.

On Sunday evening, we sit on the balcony watching the sun slip through the tangle of high tension wires. The ocean is four miles away—sometimes you can smell it if the wind overpowers the scent of the recycling bins in the alley.

"How will you know?" Kiki asks me after her third bubble catches a breeze and makes it to the center of the street before bursting into iridescent nothing.

"How will I know what?" I say, dipping my wand into the economy-sized soap vat.

"How will you know when you've met the one?'

About this, I have no doubts. All those love quizzes in the magazines Kiki brings me (*Nine Ways to Tell if He*

REALLY Cares, Five Signs He's Cheating on You) have helped me distill my own quiz down to one simple question: *Do you one-hundred-percent trust him to perform an emergency tracheotomy on you if the situation demands it?*

I tell this to Kiki, who shakes her head.

"Think about it," I say. "You're lying there, bee-stung, in the road, no epi-pen, throat swelling shut . . .."

Kiki says, "You know I'm not allergic to bees."

"Fine. You're lying there on the floor of a restaurant, choking on a meatball . . .."

"Why wouldn't you just do the Heimlich maneuver?"

"I tried that already. It didn't work."

Kiki dips her bubble wand into the soap.

"You're choking on the floor, you can't breathe, your eyes are locked on your boyfriend's face as he kneels over you. Your boyfriend snatches a pen from the waiter's apron. His thumb is on your throat, you're turning blue. You nod, eyes wide, he raises the pen . . .."

"Wouldn't a knife work better?" Kiki interrupts, then blows. A bubble bulges from the end of her wand and breaks free.

"He tosses the pen aside, grabs a steak knife off some guy's plate. He rushes back to you. You start to fade into blackness, he raises the knife and . . .."

"Score!" Kiki says, "My bubble hit the rooftop! Take a drink, loser!"

I feel a tickle start in my throat, I try to unwrap a cough drop silently but Kiki catches me.

"Hey!" she says, frowning and tilting her chair away from mine. "You're not getting sick again are you?"

The ocean breeze cuts through the alley for just a minute, bringing a whiff of salt and vastness, the promise of true love waiting with steak knife in hand.

I tell Kiki the truth. I've never been better.

Heidi Espenscheid Nibbelink is Midwestern by birth, Western by heart, and Southern by circumstance. She is earning an MFA at the Sewanee School of Letters. Her stories have been published in *Fiction Southeast, Defenestration, Drunk Monkeys,* and other journals.

Read more at heidinibbelink.com, or follow her on Twitter @AnnoyedOboist.

Chris Coulson

Put a Dollar in the Kitty

Down in Little Tokyo, I sat on a bench inside the mall because it was 110 Los Angeles degrees outside. I read the news. It was the usual news, of course. Politicians saying dull filtered careful sentences about everything getting better while the rest of us shoot at each other and drink too much and watch too much TV because we have a feeling they're lying about that.

If we have any feeling left at all.

But I shouldn't say we. This is just how I was feeling early that day, and then a woman sat down with me.

She sat down on the bench with me, right next to me, very close. I kept reading but now the news wasn't important anymore. What I was reading was just paper, nothing more, but she was so close to me I could hear her breathing in and out, I could feel her trembling, and I saw that between her black toes there was bleeding. Her shoulder was nearly touching mine, she smelled wet. We didn't look at each other. I kept reading my bits of paper.

Her labored breathing was knocking the breath out of me and she didn't seem to be able to move anymore, except for the shaking. I was wearing sunglasses so I could look at her out of the corner of my eye, thinking she wouldn't see me. But when I looked at her out of the corner of my shaded eye, I saw that she had already turned and was looking right at me. And she seemed to be ready to say something.

"I just can't take this anymore."

And that was it. She had exhaled this statement as much as she'd said it, and there wasn't really anything else for either of us to say. What she said hung in the air like smoke that wouldn't blow away. We looked away from each other in different directions.

As painful a line as that was, I started smiling, I was almost laughing. I saw that a mall security guard was watching us. I could see him out of the corner of my other shaded eye. "That fucker can go to hell," I wanted to say to the woman, but instead I superficially talked about the weather. "It's so goddamn hot out there."

I saw she was wearing a gold cross around her neck. She straightened up on the bench hearing this and now she was smiling too.

"It is goddamn hot. GODDAMN hot!" She said this much louder than I had and she slapped my leg.

I saw the security guard had turned away but was watching our reflections in the window of the Hello Kitty shop across the way. He was a tidy young cop, his shirt all tucked in, gun polished, and I guess he was watching us because she was the only Black woman in the mall and I was wearing my Keith Richards for President t-shirt. And we were sitting together. And now the conversation had moved from the weather to God, though we felt less damned.

"Do you have somewhere to go?" I asked. Right away I felt bad for asking.

"I haven't thought that far ahead yet, honey." The way she said this let me know she hadn't noticed I'd asked an idiot question. And anyway, she was staring back at the guard's reflected window face. She gave me a soft elbow bump in the ribs. "Honey, you have any spare change to help me out with? To cool me down with, if you know what I mean?"

I pulled out two twenties, stood up, took her moist, trembling hand and kissed the back of it. I put the bills in her hand and walked away.

"God*DAMN*!" I heard her say once more as I was floating up the escalator. Then, "*HELLO* Kitty!"

Chris Coulson was a bartender, morgue attendant and obituary writer (simultaneously!), newspaper reporter and actor before writing his first novel, *Nothing Normal in Cork*, followed by his first collection of poetry, *The Midwest Hotel*. His second novel, *Red Jumbo*, will be out in 2018. Visit Chris at chriscoulson.net.

Jessica Jones
The Williams Sisters and the Curios Incident

Valda and Joan lived on Greenfields. They loved it. They lived in number 94, which was all the way down the bottom, near where the street opened out into Coopers Field, where they enjoyed exploring. It was a good job as well, because with the amount of people at home, getting out was a necessity sometimes and with Valda and Joan being the youngest, they could escape easily without being noticed. It wasn't enough that out of the six children, four of them still lived at home with mum and dad; their mum often took people in—down-on-their-luck types—and gave them a place to stay. Plus, this weekend their sister Vi was coming home for a few days from her workplace in London, so that meant even more cramped living conditions.

The next day Vi was due to arrive, so they promised their mum that they would help make the house clean and tidy. Valda and Joan spent all day polishing the brass, sweeping the hearth, cleaning the windows and folding the laundry. The last task was to move the bedrooms around to create space for Vi. Their mum said that since she'd been in London this past year she couldn't be expected to share a bedroom with anyone. This was difficult because Valda, Joan and their older sister Kath already shared one bedroom, but with some jiggling they managed to move their older brother Stanley in with 'Uncle Austin' (the latest acquisition!) just for a few days to free up a room for Vi.

They were moving the last of Stanley's things through, when Joan knocked Uncle Austin's huge suitcase over with a load bang and it flew open. They both gasped, and listened…no movement came from downstairs, thank goodness. They really didn't want to be told off today. The suitcase looked empty apart from a small tatty piece of material with funny writing on it that had fallen out. Valda and Joan didn't know what Uncle Austin did during the day. He didn't leave for work like their dad did and he was always at the house when they got in from school. Sometimes he would go out at night, but most of the time he seemed to have his nose in a great big book, with a title they didn't even understand.

They had heard their dad saying that he should put the book down and go with him to the pits to do an honest day's work. Joan had once said that she didn't think he'd manage it; as he wasn't strong like their dad. She got a clip around the ear for that one!

Joan picked up the piece of material.

Valda whispered, "Don't Joan, put it back…you'll get us into trouble." Joan was always getting them into trouble, she was easily the naughtiest of the siblings.

The writing wasn't anything they'd learned in school; it looked like a foreign language. Joan sounded out the letters…and suddenly the whole room shook. Running up the stairs came Uncle Austin, wide-eyed and red in the face! He grabbed the two girls and pushed them backwards, outside the door, just as a large purple hole appeared where Joan had been standing. The wind was whipping around the room, Uncle Austin was shouting back at Joan, "How did you do that?"

Joan shrugged and held up the piece of material she had read from. Uncle Austin looked shocked.

"The missing piece!!" he shouted above the noise. "I've been looking for that for two months." He grabbed it from Joan, turned, picked up his book from the bedside table, grinned at them…and jumped!! Through the hole he went and immediately the room stopped shaking and the wind stopped howling; and he was gone.

They stood in shock. Where had he gone? What just happened? Downstairs the back door opened, and they could hear Dad and Vi arriving.

Valda panicked. "What are we going to say to Mum and Dad?"

They knew they needed to go downstairs immediately.

Joan turned at the door and hissed, "Don't say anything, we didn't see anything." Then she noticed something under the bed. It looked like that same piece of tatty material—it must have slipped from Uncle Austin's hands as his jumped. She made a mental note to retrieve it before bedtime. She wouldn't tell Valda though, not yet. She hadn't quite decided what she would do with it.

Jessica Jones is from Leicestershire, England. She is married and has been dealing with infertility for five years. She loves to write and raise awareness of infertility issues. She has had a number of articles published online and is keen to write a book about her experiences.

Visit the author at www.infertilityandlife.wordpress.com.

Old First Church, Beninngton, VT © Jackie Anthony

Anne Anthony

Hope

> *"Hope, O my soul, hope.*
> *You know neither the day nor the hour."*
>
> —St. Teresa of Avila

Daddy married against his Mama's wishes. She prayed he'd serve God as a Catholic priest. The family tells the story of when he sliced off the tip of his index finger cutting carrots. My grandmother ran cold water to stop the bleeding, panicked when the rush of water flushed the flap of skin into a sink full of leftover minestrone soup.

"He can't hold the Eucharist if it's not reattached," she kept repeating while searching through the skins of cannellini beans.

I believed he chose his daughters' names to appease his mother. My name is Hope. My sisters, Faith and Charity, changed their names after Daddy died. I liked my name, always have, but more so when I received my diagnosis the day after I turned sixty.

I first noticed the pea-sized lump on my neck last winter. I denied my body's changes: the drag of my breasts towards my belly, tags of skin on my back, and the deep creases by my eyes when I'm not smiling. Sixty is a prickly age for women. We lose our children to work or to spouses; some lose their husbands to younger women or heart attacks. Since I had neither, I felt spared.

The pea grew to the size of a walnut under the heat of summer. Dr. Wilson's eyes widened when I took off my silky scarf.

"What the hell?" Her profanity surprised me. She was a church-going woman. She ordered testing. Two days later, her office called to schedule an appointment.

—*Dr. Wilson wants to review the test results.*

The office manager spoke in a tone reserved for funerals. I prepared for bad news.

—*Salivary Cancer. Spread through the lymph system.*

Cancer wasn't new to me. My mother battled breast cancer for five years while the disease crumbled a body worthy of Michelangelo's chisel. I thanked Dr. Wilson after listening for an hour and told her I'd be on my way.

—*On your way? You need to decide on your treatment. Start this week."*

Dr. Wilson and I grew up a block from each other. We were never friends. Her father was a doctor; my Dad delivered their mail. A block of cement pavement separated our community like a border wall.

—Katie, I know how cancer works. Think you'd remember. Only two years since Mama died.

I enjoyed using her first name. Believed it leveled her. Katie and I spent eight years together at St. Martha's Parish School. Eighth grade split the class. Families with money went to private high schools; those without went to public schools. Going to college, if you were lucky enough to go to college, split us again between public and private schools of higher education. My book-learning ended in the twelfth grade.

The year I turned nineteen I discovered my knack for art. Giant sculptures fashioned from scrap metal. A lucrative business. I'm told my designs make stunning backdrops for elegant lawn parties, but I couldn't say for sure since I've never been invited. The split persisted.

I stood, shook her hand, and felt surprised by its tremble. Never crossed my mind how a person felt delivering life-ending news.

—Think I'll travel. Check out the Pacific Ocean.

I sold my house, my studio, my sculptures—finished or unfinished—and signed a month-to-month lease on an oceanfront condo. I spent mornings on my deck watching dolphins swimming east. They swam west at the end of the day. I appreciated their predictability.

My lump was the size of a walnut when I named her Sophia. Greek for wisdom. Her name pressed through my sleep like contractions and startled me awake. The name suited her like mine suited me.

Our lives fell into a comfortable rhythm. Every morning, I measured Sophia's growth like Mama once marked my height on the doorjamb to the basement. I drew rings around her, bursts of colorful concentric circles reminiscent of Kandinsky's abstract brushstrokes. Every evening, we sat outdoors, and I told her stories. Whenever I repeated Daddy's mishap with the knife, I felt her tingle. Sophia was laughing, I told myself.

When she grew to the size of a lime, I rang up my lawyer to change my will. Over breakfast, before the dolphins swam east, I reassured my Sophia. No one would slice her off my dead body like the tip of Daddy's finger. When we'd go, we'd go together.

Anne Anthony has been published in the *North Carolina Literary Review, Brilliant Flash Fiction, Dead Mule School for Southern Literature, Poetry South,* and elsewhere. She holds a Masters in Professional Writing from Carnegie Mellon University. She lives and writes full-time in North Carolina.

"Reading gave me hope. For me, it was the open door."

—Oprah Winfrey

Shadow Man © Anne Anthony

John Baltisberger
Highway Severance

I was driving down I-10 heading towards Houston when I felt the rhythmic thumping of the flat tire. Immediately, amidst great amounts of profanity, I pulled off onto the shoulder of the road and sat behind the wheel. Texas highways were not the best place to experience car trouble. The distance between cities and towns was insurmountable by foot, and the weather, even in the fall, was sweltering. To top it all off I was in a nice rental. The tire should not be flat.

My music still blaring, I considered my options. I could try to call someone, though it was unlikely anyone would be close enough to do anything, and hell, a tow truck would cost a fortune just to get to the nearest shop. I could change the tire myself, but that was assuming that the spare was in the trunk, I didn't want to get my suit dirty before my meeting and, even if both of those things passed muster, I would still have to drive quite a distance on that spare. Even calling roadside assistance seemed like a shitty idea honestly.

I was mulling these ideas over when I felt it again.

Thump. Thump. Thump. The sound of the flat tire hitting the road, while the car was sitting still. I turned off the music, and then the engine. If this was an engine issue, I was going to tear those rental guys a new hole. I would certainly miss my meeting in that case, and now I had to call a tow. I wouldn't even know where to begin looking for the problem. Luckily, with apps, calling the tow involved just a few swipes of the. . .

THUMP. THUMP. THUMP.

My blood ran cold. The engine was off, there was no movement in the car, other than the slight reverberations from the sound of something thumping in the trunk. A wild animal. Was I going to open the trunk to find some sort of rabid dog or a deranged raccoon with an attitude problem? I opened the door and slid out of the car slowly. I took several steps away, trying to decide what to do, I could always wait for the tow truck to get here. I wouldn't have to worry about dealing with whatever was going on myself. That didn't sound great. It made me look like a coward for one.

Shaking my head, trying to deny the insanity of the situation, I moved to the back of the car. It was sweltering out here; whatever was in the trunk would be way too hot to be dangerous. Occasionally, it thumped again, too loud to be a raccoon, had to be some sort of dog that had slipped in while the cleaners weren't paying attention. It was the only thing that made sense.

Taking a deep breath, I popped the trunk. As soon as it started to swing open, there was a huge noise, like the crack of thunder, and something hit my chest knocking me off my feet onto the hot highway pavement. I touched my chest. It felt like I had been hit by a hammer, but when I looked at my hand, it was covered in blood. I was bleeding. I couldn't breathe, and a nasty sucking noise was coming from my chest every time I tried.

Getting out of my trunk, as though it was the most normal place for him to be, was a dark man in a suit. Gun in hand, he looked me over, as though appraising his work. Maybe that was what he was doing.

"You John?" I couldn't get enough air to answer, so I just nodded. "Well, thank God for that."

He gave me the kind of smile you give someone when you're sharing a crappy moment that can't be helped, before reaching into his pocket and reading from a note card. "Your services at Universal Sales are no longer required, as your position has been terminated." He put the card back into his coat pocket. "Some people just don't want to pay severance. Sorry, buddy."

This was a mistake, I sold cured meat products for God's sake. I wasn't a gangster. But the noon sky was already getting dark, all my senses were going grey as I watched the man, whoever he was, get in my rental car and drive away.

John Baltisberger works on writing and world building for games, but in his free time loves to write short horror inspired by the works of Robert Howard and Ashton Clark Smith. *Highway Severance* was inspired by his own layoff, which at the end of the day was a blessing.

Stop by for a visit: SouthernFriedStories.wordpress.com.

Carina Stopenski
Creek Dreams

You gonna keep it?" Van's voice was muffled, his lower lip packed with Skoal. He traced his finger on Leah's stomach in a circular motion before she turned over onto her side.

She pulled her faded Lynyrd Skynyrd t-shirt over the small bloat in her stomach and stretched her legs across the mattress. Van's trailer was on the border of town, right by the bank of the creek, and the bedroom was more of a glorified closet. The two of them were wedged on the twin-sized bed together, half for intimacy and half for warmth.

"Course I'm gonna. It's my body, ain't it? If it's my body, it's my baby." Leah popped her gum and wedged a pillow between her legs. "What'd you think of Daisy if it's a girl? I like Daisy."

"You gonna tell Benji?" Van stared at the ceiling before letting out a sigh.

"Well, I'm gonna have to, you know? He'll think it's his. They all will." She pointed a finger. "And he's gonna go to his grave thinking it's his, you got that? He and I have been together for a long time, Van. Ain't gonna screw up how much me and him have gone through just 'cause you and I got handsy one night." Leah's voice trembled, and Van couldn't tell if it was anger or fear causing the tremor.

"I don't see why you can't say it's mine. Or not even have it. You really wanna raise a baby out in the boonies? All we got here are creeks, farms, and the drugstore. You want a baby having to walk three miles to school every day?"

Leah laughed. "A baby ain't gonna have to walk, Van. Babies don't go to school."

"That's not what I mean, Leah," Van answered. "I meant when that baby grows up. You want that baby living in Deer Rock? No. This ain't no place to start a family."

"My family's here," Leah said. "Your family's here. Benji's family and all of our friends from school. We're all here. You saying we ain't got good families?"

Van caught himself. "Not what I meant, Leah. Just, you're seventeen. You're still a baby too. You think you can go through two more years of school with a kid?"

"Maybe I won't even do school no more." Leah shrugged, readjusting the bottom hem of her shirt as it rode up over her baby bump.

"The hell with that! And what? You gonna end up like Benji's sister. You gonna pump out three kids and have a husband that leaves you before twenty-five? That ain't no way to live, Leah. I'd be good to you. I'd take you somewhere new. Hell, maybe we could make it to Charleston. Me, you, and the baby. We could all load up in my truck and drive for miles. You could go to one of those nice public schools in the city, the ones with daycare in them for the baby. I could get a job helping fix the roads or holding them signs at construction sites, you know? They get paid a lot."

Leah sighed. "What happens when I get big, you know? From the baby?"

"You mean gain weight? Hell, you'll still be pretty to me. You could be two pounds or two thousand pounds, you'll still be gorgeous. Shit, Leah. You act like I ain't loved you since kindergarten."

"Then how come you left me?"

"What you mean, 'left you'? You mean how I finished school?"

"Yeah."

"Girl, I finished school because I never got left back a grade. I pulled my ass out of bed and did what I could. You act like they held you back 'cuz they wanted to. You barely go. You think having a baby's gonna make it easier? That you gonna get special treatment? Teachers out here don't even know math that good. Out in the city, they treat you good. They help you if you having trouble. They send your work home so you can do it when you get sick. It could be good for us. Hell, I could go to college!"

"You really think so?"

"I know so." Van pressed his hand against Leah's cheek and rested his head next to hers. "You ain't as dumb as you think you are. You got smarts. What'd you say we do this?"

"And leave Benji?"

"Well, Benji ain't here right now, is he? I am. I got us into this mess, so I'm gonna get us out, okay?"

Leah smiled. "What about Jacob for a boy?"

"Yeah, yeah. I like Jacob. That's a good one." Van shifted up and spat his tobacco in the trash can before kissing the crown of Leah's head. "You wanna go for a dip in the creek?"

"Have you ever heard me say no anytime with you?"

Carina Stopenski is a BFA student of Creative Writing at Chatham University. Her work has been published in or is forthcoming in *The Honey Bee Review*, *Cold Creek Review*, *Impossible Archetype*, and *Life in 10 Minutes*, among others, as well as the anthology, *Pennsylvania's Best Emerging Poets*.

"Books can be dangerous.
The best ones should be labeled
'This could change your life.'"

—Helen Exley

Brightthelmston Eye © Stephen Moore

Cathleen O'Connor
The Vapors

As soon as Jim stepped out of the car, a head of blond curls and flailing arms hurtled towards him.

"Pop-pa!" Lily shrieked as she wrapped her arms around his knees. "Pop-pa, you're here!"

Jim picked her up, balancing her bumble bee clad bottom on his arm and pressed his nose to hers. Nose kisses were their thing ever since she learned about Eskimos in pre-school. Her little nose wiggled back and forth against his and she sighed.

"Pop-pa, it's been too long." Lily exaggerated her words and 'too' went on and on. Like how she said poppa. It was never just one word. It was always first 'pop' followed by a pause and then a completely distinct 'pa.' Like she took a breath in-between.

"How ya been puddin? Keepin ya ma busy?"

"She sure has." His daughter Sally was smiling as she walked up to them and pressed a kiss to his cheek. "How are ya Pop?"

"Right as rain, darlin," Jim said, "especially when I'm with my girls."

"Pop-pa!" Lily grabbed his chin and turned his face back to her. "Can we go to Dukies for ice cream later?"

"Dukies it is, puddin, but first I have a real surprise for ya." Lily's eyes looked like they were going to burst out of her face. "What surprise Pop-pa? What surprise?"

"Well . . .," Jim turned to look at Sally. "Mickey and Minnie are visitin Hillsborough today." Lily's body jerked so hard that Jim almost dropped her.

"Here?" she shrieked. "Mickey is here?"

"Yup, puddin. He's here. Puttin on a show at the convention center and . . .." Jim paused for effect. "I got us a ticket to meet Mickey in person."

"Pop-Pa!" Lily grabbed his face in both her hands and slammed her nose into his. "Ow!" they both said at the same time. "What will I wear? Mama, what will I wear? It's Mickey!" Sally detected the note of panic creeping into Lily's voice.

"No worries, Lily-bug. Mama has it under control. I pressed your pink frilly skirt and laid out your purple leggings and your favorite sparkly tee. Mickey is gonna be dazzled."

Lily's butt wiggled on Jim's arm. "Put me down Pop-pa. I gotta get ready." As soon as her feet hit the pavement she was off running into the house.

Sally looked at Jim. "Ya sure ya know what ya gettin into here, Pop? The shriek meter's gonna be off the charts."

Jim winked and hugged his daughter. "Just like her mama was at that Backstreet Boys concert."

The convention hall was outside the center of town and Jim could already see the line of cars waiting to get into the lot. Lily was pretty much bouncing non-stop in her booster seat in the back, chattering away to Jim and watching her favorite Mickey Mouse Club videos on her iPad.

"Now puddin, ya not gonna get the vapors, are ya when ya meet Mickey?" Lily looked at him in the rearview mirror.

"What are vapors, Pop-pa?"

"Well Lily-bug, when a Southern woman meets the man of her dreams, sometimes she almost faints from the excitement. That's what we call gettin the vapors."

"That's silly, Pop-pa." Lily giggled.

The big moment finally arrived. The show was over, and Lily was one person away from meeting Mickey and Minnie. Mickey was first. Whoever was doing the character today was good. His voice sounded exactly like the high-pitched Mickey of the movies.

"Well, hi there sweetheart. What's your name?" Mickey bent down to take Lily's hand. To Jim's surprise Lily didn't answer, her big eyes staring up at Mickey.

"Uh, this is my sweet Lily-bug," Jim found himself saying to Mickey.

"Lily. What a pretty name for a pretty girl," Mickey said. "Thanks for coming to meet me and Minnie." And with that they were ushered off to the gift bag table.

On the ride home Jim kept glancing in the rearview mirror. Lily was sitting in her booster seat with her eyes closed. "Puddin? Ya okay?"

"Shhh, Pop-pa," Lily spoke softly, "I'm makin a memory."

"Well, how'd it go?" Sally asked.

Lily crooked her finger at her mother so she'd bend down to her. "I got the vapors, Mama." Lily whispered. "I got the vapors when I met Mickey."

"Ya did?" Sally asked. She looked up at her father. He was standing with his arms crossed and his eyes closed. "Pop, ya must be tired."

"Shhh, darling. Not tired. I'm makin a memory."

Cathleen O'Connor PhD is a writer, speaker, teacher, coach and intuitive who offers editing, publishing, book-layout and marketing services to other writers. Author of the bestselling book, *365 Days of Angel Prayers.* She has been quoted in the *Huffington Post* on dreams and blogs regularly for numerologist.com.

Learn more: www.cathleenoconnor.com.

Exultation © Tricia Leaf

"I admire writers, the other half of the brain, however, I find the strongest way to communicate is with a camera and made it my profession. An effective photo tells a story in one glance and I do love telling stories."
—P. Decker

Photography credits on facing page from top to bottom: **Sweetheart © P. Decker, What's Out There? © Judy Guenther Photography, Her Eyes © Judy Guenther Photography, and Cards © P. Decker.**

139

Karen Thrower
Bingo!

R ay sat on the wooden stool in front of the ancient
cardboard box. His father's old B-12 Bomber
airplane model. The workbench was still littered
with tools and old paint cans. He could smell oil and glue
and metal. Smells reminding him of his father. He
opened the dusty lid and inside he saw the half-finished
model plane.

He remembered when they started it. Ray was ten
years old, and more interested in playing outside than
hunkering over a model plane in the basement for hours.
They only managed to put the propellers on before he
started complaining—*I want to go outside, Dad! This is
boring!* —he remembered telling his father. He didn't
realize it at the time, but Dad just wanted to spend time
together. Ray had no idea they'd never finish it.

Ray picked up the tiny scissors out of a nearby drawer
and started snipping the pieces off the plastic.

"What were they called?" he asked talking out loud to
himself as he snipped. "A real, funny word." He finished
snipping a wing off when he remembered. "Sprues!" He

laughed. "That's right, what an odd word."

He laid all the pieces out and made sure they were still there. He clapped once. "All there! Okay."

He unfolded the instructions and pulled a tube of plastic cement out of a clear drawer in front of him.

"Man, this stuff smelled awful." He opened it up and squeezed the tube, making sure it wasn't dried out. A huge glob squirted out. "Oh crap!"

He grabbed a nearby rag and started wiping it off the workbench. The last thing he wanted was his arms to get stuck to it with his cell phone out of reach. Ray fixed the glue tube and picked up one of the wings. "Okay, here we go."

He worked for hours, making sure every piece fit perfect into another. He glued the wheels on and held it up. "Not bad if I say so."

He noticed the little jars of paint above the workbench.

"What do you say to a new coat of paint?" he asked the bomber. "White and red, you say? I think we can do that." He put his mother's wooden clothespins on the wheel joints and put the plane down on the workbench. He found red, white and black paint which settled at the bottom. With a little shake their color came back to life.

Ray opened the drawer where his father kept his paint brushes and found three small ones perfect for the bomber. He carefully painted a red stripe around it, and put a black one above it. He took the white paint and painted the wings and the tip, making sure not to smudge the drying paint. "Bingo!"

He gently blew on plane, remembering how his dad did the same thing. He had wondered why he didn't just let the thing sit and dry, but now he knew. He felt his Dad's excitement in finishing his model, how he wanted the plane to dry quicker.

Ray leaned back and looked at the finished model.

"Looks pretty good." He looked up a black and white photo of Dad and him that his father kept for years above his workbench. Mom took the picture of the two of them together. He was around four when his dad helped him learn how to ride his tricycle. "Doesn't it, Dad?"

Karen Thrower is a native Oklahoman, wife, and mother to a rambunctious four-year old. She holds a Bachelor's degree in Deaf Education from The University of Tulsa. She is also a member of Oklahoma Science Fiction Writers and serves as the Vice-President and Facebook 'Wizard'.

"A story is what it's like
to be a human being—
to be knocked down
and to miraculously arise.
Each one of us
has arisen, awakened.
We do rise."
—Maya Angelou

Legs © P. Decker

Julie Eger
Reining in the Storm

K yree! Where are you?" Maxine's hands shot to her hips. Her eyes flashed, scanning the long driveway for the five-year-old. A storm was brewing and by the looks of the leaves whirling on the trees, it was going to be a dandy even by Wisconsin standards. Her forefathers had a good reason for branding this windswept prairie Tornado Alley. Right now that reason was bubbling like a hot pot of chili inside her gut.

"Kyree!"

"I'm over here. By Leopold!"

"What on earth?" Maxine twisted around and headed for the corral. Her breath hitched in her throat. "Kyree. Keep still. Oh good lord, he's going to step on you!"

The skin along Leopold's forequarters twitched off a swarm of storm flies as the big horse pawed the ground in front of him. There was nothing nastier than a fly before a storm. They bit hard and deep. Leopold's hoof grazed the air an inch from Kyree's head.

"He won't step on me. I asked him if it was alright to sit underneath him. He said it was okay."

"Honey, draft horses can't talk. Leopold weighs a ton. One wrong move and he'll crush you."

"No, he won't. We made a deal." Leopold pounded a back hoof, pile-driving it into the ground. The flies scattered but sucked right back onto his leg like black magnets. Kyree glanced at the hole in the ground next to her foot. "See, he won't hurt me." Kyree lifted Grandpa's old pan flute to her lips and began to blow a string of abstract notes. "Leopold likes my music. He said I could help him rein in this storm. We're going to unwind it."

"Honey, come out from under there. Leopold needs to find a safe place to stay in the pasture until this storm blows over."

A gust of wind crashed through the bottleneck between the house and barn, dragging their old tom cat backwards, claws scratching for purchase on the cement surrounding the pump house as the blades on the windmill screeched overhead.

"I know. He'll go by the big oak tree. He'll back up to it and then stick his nose into the wind. That's how he can tell what the storm is going to do. Then I'm going to play my flute. Don't fret, Grandma. We've got this, even if it is my very first time. Leopold said he'd tell me what to do then he'll do the rest." Kyree jumped up and raced toward the gate just as Leopold jack-hammered both legs to rid himself of the angry flies. The gate swung open and Leopold hightailed it out of the corral heading toward the tree. A gust of wind knocked Kyree sideways, but she held fast to the flute.

Maxine scooped her up in one swoop and headed for the house. The wind drove dust into her lungs and she coughed it out. Kyree swiped her hand across her eyes and yelled, "I need to play my flute!"

"Kyree, we've got to get in the basement..." A brown mountain mushroomed up over the tops of the trees on the back forty. Maxine recognized it as the funnel working itself into a full blown twister. "Holy Jesus!"

Kyree wrenched free of her grandmother's grasp. She hit the ground running, headed back toward the corral.

"I've got to play my flute!" Kyree screamed. "Leopold is counting on me!" She jumped up and wound her arms and legs through the slats, locking herself onto the gate. "Leopold said if he spins headfirst toward the silo I'm to play the first song. If he spins toward the chicken coop I'm to play the second song."

Maxine fought through a gust of choking dust. She watched in horror as the brown cloud full of lightning bolts started twisting toward her granddaughter.

"Kyree you'll never..."

Kyree focused on Leopold. She caught a glimpse of him through the swirling dust. Her little fingers wrapped around the flute. Leopold backed up to the oak tree, stuck his nose into the wind. Then he galloped out into the pasture and pulled a double kicker like a guaranteed champion in a South Dakota rodeo, spinning headfirst toward the chicken coop. Kyree's lips puckered against the mouth of the flute and a melody, lovely and haunting as anything Maxine had ever heard, pierced the air. Reining in the lightning bolts, the twister, her heart.

After learning the art of dowsing from the yokels, **Julie Eger** now keeps busy writing stories and forcing the few friends she has to read them. She is currently working on a spell to rid people of their addictions to sex. Her work can be found on Amazon.

Visit her website at: julieceger.wordpress.com.

Nina Fortmeyer
Swap

I don't recognize the key in my hand. I don't recognize my hand either. It's a fair hand like a white lady's, and shaking so hard, I can't make the key meet the oak door in front of me. I take a deep breath and try again. Come on. Again. Finally.

I slide in quick, before anyone sees I'm out of my cell.

The crystal chandelier hanging over the foyer sparkles in the light slanting through high windows, and I know this gets cleaned regularly. Glad it's not me up on a ladder doing it, not this time. Been there, done that, got the cleaning rag.

There are no guards in sight.

I creep through the mansion silently, past the darkened formal living room to the part of the house where people would live. A tanned fit white man with dark curly hair sprawls on a gray leather couch drinking a beer, watching football on a giant TV. I pinch myself. It hurts.

The forgotten front door slams itself shut. I press myself against a wall, waiting, silent except for my heartbeat. On the TV, someone throws a long pass. The young man leans forward.

"Hey Hon, I picked up dinner," he says, never taking his eyes off the screen.

"Thanks."

The word rolls off my tongue like I grew up speaking English. I quickly slide out of the room, following a garlicky aroma to a fancy gourmet kitchen like the ones I used to clean. Not like the little corner kitchen I fed my whole family out of, back before I got sent away. This one is set up for big catered parties, with hot boxes and a giant glass front fridge. Custom.

The counters are lower than normal. Even the deep sink with the arched pewter faucet is low. No, it's me. I'm taller somehow, with long legs wearing tight leather boots. Real leather. Breathing fast, I look for the half bath that's always near the kitchen in expensive houses, the one the help uses.

In a burgundy-walled wine room, I find a framed copy of that famous painting where Texas steals itself from Mexico, only that's not how the painter sees it. He shows the invaders as winners, not thieves, like they had a right to take everything.

The laundry room is bigger than my cell. And safer. I don't know what will happen when they see I'm gone. I'm afraid to try the next door, in case it takes me back.

It's cracked a little. Not enough to let me see in. There is no light. I open it slowly. Grope for the switch.

Score. The marble sink shines like money, but it's the pewter-framed mirror calling me. Heart jumping out of my chest, I make myself look. And nearly choke.

I wink. Sallie Marveaux winks back at me. Sallie, the beautiful thief who framed her office's cleaning service. The liar whose time I'm serving.

Was serving.

I help myself to a slice of pizza, open an imported beer and join the hunk on the couch.

Nina Fortmeyer is a pastry chef from Nashville, where she is a volunteer with Killer Nashville Writers Conference and active in Nashville Writers Meetup. Her writing has appeared in *Nashville Noir, Everyday Fiction, Origami Journal, Rose Red Review* and *101 Words*. Her story *SHADOW* won a local award.

Leedville Sign © Suzi Banks Baum

Norm Titterington
One Night Only

The ancient marquee displayed the announcement as well as it possibly could with only half its lamps still functional. SPECIAL ENGAGEMENT— FRANKIE FALCON, TONIGHT, 7 P.M. SHOW!

The Blue Door Lounge welcomed the return of an old friend; a legendary performer, but one who hadn't played there in many years. The elderly bluesman gave a brief wave to the sparse crowd and shuffled toward the chair and microphone at the center of the stage. Franklin Brown's weathered visage mimicked the well-worn hardwood planks of the platform as he sat down and prepared to revive the club's dormant live music history.

The lounge opened the day after Prohibition was repealed, and for decades was considered the premier "colored musicians club" in the entire state. At its peak, that hand-crafted oak stage hosted all the great blues musicians of the day. T-Bone Walker appeared several times in the late 1930s, Lead Belly and Lightnin' Hopkins performed on glorious back-to-back nights in '41, and John Lee Hooker scorched the stage at least a dozen times in the '50s and '60s.

And then there was Franklin Roosevelt Brown. He hit the Blue Door stage for the first time in 1967 as a cocky nineteen-year-old with a passion for classic electric blues and a nimble set of fingers that alternated between strumming subtle riffs and lighting the guitar's fretboard ablaze with ferocious leads. He earned his performance moniker when a newspaper reviewer opined about his guitar solos "soaring like the majestic falcon in flight."

Frankie Falcon created such a following among blues enthusiasts in the area that he became the house act at the Blue Door and packed the club weekly for over twenty-five years. But desire for live music faded as the neighborhood grew younger and musical tastes changed. Eventually it was once a month, then once every few months, and by 1997 it had been over a year since Frankie had graced the venerable stage. Occasionally, a local artist might perform a set or two at the lounge, but most evenings the once-distinguished club was reduced to a few regulars drinking half-priced beer and well drinks while the jukebox in the corner wore out the same blues and classic rock tunes it had been playing every night for almost twenty years.

But perhaps tonight would be different. Frankie Falcon was tuning his guitar and getting ready for his return to the spotlight, over thirteen years after his "farewell" show back in his hometown of Calumet City.

The first awkward chords elicited some laughter from the patrons at the bar as Frankie warmed up for a few moments. Nodding to the house band behind him, he looked out front and thanked the tiny crowd for attending, launching into his opening number, a powerful take on the B.B. King classic, *How Blue Can You Get?* His gravelly voice showed his age, but his fingers glided over the guitar strings as though he was permanently in 1979. The laughter faded, and a reverent hush fell over the club, followed by the low din of phones being activated; friends, family, and even mere acquaintances being called or texted to hurry over and join the moment. Something special was happening, and everyone knew it needed to be shared. In a short time, the crowd swelled toward a size well beyond legal capacity—the legendary club was alive once again.

When he soared into his first solo of the night, the enormous gathering of blues fans erupted in wild applause, reveling in the intensity and pure, magical joy of this near-religious musical experience. Frankie Falcon had brought the Blue Door Lounge to its collective feet, and he basked in the glow of the spotlight as the extended solo break came to climax in front of a thunderous crowd. The young concertgoers may have been discovering Frankie Falcon for the first time, but Franklin Brown was re-discovering his prime and his passion for the music. He was twenty again; and the entire club joined in the ecstatic moment.

Norm Titterington is a writer whom no one has heard of. He's OK with that for the time being. He's also a late-life college graduate, a dad, a husband, a coach, and a lover of music and chicken wings...not always in that order.

Charles Leipart
The Sleep of the Righteous

*S*am?

What?

Are you awake?

I am now.

I can't sleep. I'm having this recurring dream.

Try reading. Reading always does it for me. Puts me right out.

It's this dream, Sam. It keeps coming back and waking me. Can I tell it?

We won't sleep until you do.

In my dream we're out there.

Out where?

Out back of our country place. We're lying side by side in Mr. Boelzner's potato field.

Mr. Boelzner's field? What are we doing there?

We're lying naked. Amid rows and rows of freshly furrowed earth, just out back of our country place in Water Mill.

You said.

And old man Boelzner is on his tractor manuring and turning the soil, manuring and turning before the first frost. The blades are twisting deep, Sam, so deep—and turning, turning all that tired old soil under, and suddenly, we're turning too, Sam, and going under. Down and around we go, down and around, Sam—and now, suddenly—it's all so clear, isn't it?

It is. What is?

Our going under. We have to serve, Sam. We have to serve and replenish the earth. If only we can see ourselves as a kind of fertilizer. You and I as a very special, high-quality manure. We shall have served our purpose, Sam. Our deaths shall not have been in vain.

No. Not in vain. The light, Meg. Off, please.

We should call Bob Thomas in the morning and change our wills.

Call Bob. In the morning. Change our wills. Check the transmission on the Mercedes.

We should be cremated. And have the children take the

ashes and sprinkle them over a potato field on Long Island—preferably along the South Fork. We've had so much pleasure there, we ought to give some back as potatoes.

Potatoes?

Long Island Golds. They are indigenous there. I'd like to think of us as part of the staples of someone's diet. It's such a versatile tuber, really. There's so many ways they can serve us: creamed or baked or fried, or sliced very thin and baked in an oven for 40 minutes with some nicely grated cheese on top.

If you're hungry, get up and get something. It'll help you sleep.

As potatoes, we could best feed the poor. If they're going to eat the rich, as the graffiti in our driveway says, I think it's best if they eat us as potatoes.

Call Bob Thomas in the morning. Put it in our wills. Sprinkle us.

And seaward, Sam. The smell. We wouldn't want to offend the locals. We shall have found peace, Sam. As potatoes.

We have. Uh-huh. Taters.

I see us heaped high on some poor family's plate. Steaming. With a sprig of parsley for color. Warming a few bellies, helping young bodies grow tall and strong.

That's what it boils down to.

Ashes to ashes, dust to dust—

Dust to potatoes.

It's what we've been wanting all along, Sam. A purpose. A deep, underlying purpose to give meaning to our lives, because a life without purpose is meaningless.

It is. Meaningless. Absolutely. Your elbow.

I think I can sleep now. I'm glad I worked that out.

You did. Yeah. Did.

My sleep will be sweet. The sweet, untroubled sleep of the Righteous. Sam? Sam? Are you awake?

Charles Leipart's work has appeared in the *Bayou Magazine*, the *Jabberwock Review*, *Burningword Literary Journal*, *Panolpy Literary Zine*, and the *Eastern Iowa Review*. Charles is a graduate of Northwestern University, a former fellow of the Edward Albee Foundation. He lives and writes in New York City.

Visit Charles at: www.charlesleipart.com.

Linda Johnson
Crossing Guard

I gazed out the mini-van window as my mom drove us to school. Rain pounded the inky black pavement, drops bounced frantically into the air like BBs. The windows steamed with the breath of the five of us. My sister, an eighth-grader, commandeered the front as always. Two years younger, I sat crammed in back with two neighbor boys who smelled like week-old gym socks. We all wore Catholic school uniforms: boys in light blue shirts with navy slacks and clip-on ties; girls in navy and gray wool plaid skirts with white blouses.

Suddenly the car screeched to a stop, jolted me from my half-sleep. My mother leaped out, planted herself in the middle of the crosswalk, and held up her hand to halt traffic. She waited until the on-coming car came to a full stop, glared at the driver, her jaw clenched. Then she turned to the group of kids huddled at the side of the road, their uniforms drenched. She motioned to them.

"Come on now," she called. The kids paused, then tore across the street and bolted down the last block to the school entrance.

Mom stood in the pouring rain as more kids ran down the street toward the crosswalk. Her short brown hair, set in perfect curls before, was now plastered against her scalp. Her make-up washed down her face like an abstract painting, streaks of black mascara, blue eye shadow and pink blush. After shepherding the last group through the crosswalk, she got into our car, soaking wet and as disheveled as a lost puppy.

"Catholic school, and no one can wait a few minutes to let the children cross," she muttered, jammed the gear into drive, then slowly accelerated, watching for more kids, ready to jump into action.

I sank into my seat, mortified. Our mini-van crawled to the school entrance, its bright green doors shimmering in the rain. I unbuckled my seatbelt and grabbed my backpack.

Mom turned around, flashed a big smile as water dripped from her hair onto the car seat. "Have a good day, kids."

I ran for the school entrance, my head down, face burning. My mother always had to play hero, no matter how silly she looked. I said a quick Hail Mary that none of the cool kids had seen her.

Later that day I sat in the cafeteria eating lunch alone, trying to look invisible. Brittany, the queen bee, and the rest of the cool girls sat at the next table.

A woman walked into the lunchroom dressed in yoga pants and a headband, carrying a wet umbrella. She approached their table.

"Hey, girls."

"Hi, Mrs. Yeager." Brittany's mom. All the mothers took turns as lunch monitor.

"Sorry I'm late. You won't believe what just happened. I think I hit a dog." She dropped her umbrella on the table. "He came out of nowhere."

"Oh my God, Mom. Is he okay?" Brittany asked.

"I don't know, honey."

The girls looked at each other, horrified.

"Mom, didn't you stop to check?" Brittany's face turned a deep shade of red.

Mrs. Yeager waved her hand. "I'm sure he's fine. Some man in the car behind me stopped." She looked down at her daughter. "I didn't want to get wet."

She picked up her umbrella, said something about a meeting with the PTA president, and left the cafeteria.

One by one, the girls at the next table walked out, leaving Brittany alone. Their voices carried across the lunchroom as they slammed Mrs. Yeager.

I picked up my tray and started to leave. I thought of

my mom out in the rain this morning. If she had hit a dog, she would have taken him to the vet, paid the emergency fees, and likely adopted him if she couldn't find his owners.

I glanced at Brittany slumped back in her chair, her eyes watering. What would my mom do? I put down my tray, pulled out a chair, and sat down next to Brittany.

Linda Johnson lives in North Carolina with her husband and corgi. She has published two novels, *A Tangled Web,* and *Trail of Destruction*, and several short stories. Her most recent short story, *All Clear*, was published in the anthology, *Carolina Crimes: 21 Tales of Need, Greed and Dirty Deeds*.

Find her online at: www.LindaJohnson.us.

Eric Luthi
Refining Fire

Arriving before dawn, I scratched a shallow hole in the sand and covered it with desert camouflage netting. For all practical purposes, I was invisible. Even infra-red wouldn't pick me up. The heat would see to that. I waited.

Across the thousand yards of desert that separated us, the image of the door wavered. The heat was incredible. Water mirages came off the sand and flooded my line of sight. My eyes hurt from looking through the scope. The netting that hid me provided only broken shade and did almost nothing to ease the glare that surrounded me. There was no activity at the door set in the side of the desert mound. I rested my head against the wooden stock of my rifle.

A black beetle came marching across the sand, moving from one patch of shade to the next, approaching my hiding spot. It marched on, over rock and thorn, across the heat until it came to my rifle barrel. It stopped a quarter of an inch from the barrel and raised itself up on its short legs as if inspecting this long metal anomaly lying in the sun. Then, it abruptly changed direction, walking around the long barrel and back onto its path. Again, I waited.

I waited just like all the others waited at their own doors, waiting for him to come out. We couldn't know which door he would use, only that he would come out and it would be today. There were thousands of doors just like this one. Some set in earth, some in rock, some in concrete subway tunnels and some, like this one, in the desert. There weren't enough of us to watch them all, so we guessed the best we could and took our chances. If we got lucky, one of us might get a shot.

I heard a whisper. At first, it didn't register in my brain, it came on so slowly. The whisper got louder like a wind approaching in the trees. I looked around. Coming down out of the end of the valley were three cars. Three unmarked white sedans moving fast on the asphalt road.

The door in the mound opened inward. It was black inside. Black such that I could not see in. The sedans stopped in front of the mound and four men in dark suits and sunglasses got out of each car, twelve in all. Engines running, and doors open, they moved toward the mound.

The twelve stopped. A man emerged from the doorway. An ordinary looking man. Not at all what I expected. He had a round face and was balding and, unlike the others, didn't wear sunglasses. He moved toward the middle sedan.

The men in sunglasses parted for him as he walked toward the car. I didn't have a clear shot. One chance only to get it right, to make everything right. But, there was too much interference. Too many bodies in the way. I didn't have the shot.

He reached the second sedan and stopped at the open door. I saw his head clearly now and lined up the cross-hairs over his right ear. I stopped breathing and my finger tensed on the trigger.

He stopped, just in the act of climbing in. Then he turned, raised one eyebrow, and looked directly at me. I now saw his eyes for the first time. Brown and ordinary. Across a thousand yards of desert, through the fingers of heat rising from the sand, down through my scope, he looked at me as if looking into my soul. He looked at me for a few moments with a sadness in his eyes and then he nodded ever so slightly.

At that moment, all I could see were my own failures, my own sins, my own shame. I couldn't pull the trigger. I no longer had the right.

With no other gesture, he got into the sedan. The men in the sunglasses climbed into their cars and the three white sedans drove off.

I could only lay in the sand.

Eric Luthi is the principal of an alternative high school by day. At night, he writes and teaches at a community college. He is the father of four and husband of one. He has previously published short stories and plays.

Learn more at: ericluthi.com.

Jacklynn M Desmond
Rickets

Colorado Springs Municipal airport was buzzing with life, even at noon on a Tuesday, the place crawled with travelers, and I scanned the ones closest to us. A businessman in a wrinkled shirt and long, skinny tie. A group of rowdy teen-somethings in Day-Glo green shirts proclaiming "Jesus Saves" followed by a large, harried-looking middle-aged woman, who had the misfortune of wearing the same color. Three pretty girls in long skirts and hajibs.

As I leaned against the cream-colored column, I ignored the hajibs, or tried to, and that was progress. I congratulated myself on noticing they were pretty first, and ran my hand over my three-day beard, willing my blood pressure down. When that didn't work, I reached for my wife's hand. I focused on my daughter as she twirled in her new skirt through the patches of sunlight.

"Screen says it's on time," Anne said. She was always looped into my head, and when I was gone, her voice was a constant track on repeat. *Be safe. Come home. I love you.* She knew the real reason I was on edge.

"Nothing is ever on time in this place," I grumbled, and she answered me with a laugh.

"Is it harder on this side of the gate?" Anne asked. I kissed the top of her hair, and gave her a gentle kiss on the cheek.

"Much," I said. "I hope he's ok." It was Anne's turn to tense up, even though I knew she didn't mean to, but it irritated me. "He saved my life, Anne. He's got to go somewhere."

"I know," Anne breathed; her hand drifting to her belly as she gazed at our daughter. "I just…two little ones, Mike. War changes things. It changed you."

It did change me, and unlike my buddy, I didn't have shrapnel in my ass.

"I'm sorry," I whispered. "I'm trying."

"It's ok," she replied.

It wasn't yet, but it was getting better. My hand joined hers resting on her baby bump. So much better. I wanted to make her all kinds of promises just then, but a PFC in a crisp set of desert fatigues interrupted us.

"Cap'n Hollis?" the kid asked, snapping me a smart salute. I left Anne's side and returned the respect. It felt odd, but natural. I'd either been out too long, or not long enough.

"Sargent Rickets will be coming off the plane first; they're just getting his stuff. He's had a little something, to take the edge off."

"I was hoping he would," I said. "But not too much that he can't walk?"

"Sir?" The kid's dumbfounded look almost made me laugh, but when I spotted the military green. I broke into a run to meet him, skidding to a kneel just a foot away.

An excited yelp erupted from inside, and I unlocked the door to the camouflaged crate to let Staff Sargent Rickets, ninety pounds of German shepherd, mow me down. He knew he was home, and things were better. So much better.

Jacklynn M Desmond, a mother, author, and caregiver, lives in the "Frozen Tundra" of Northeast Wisconsin. Much of her time is spent corralling her precocious three-year-old son, the Rebel, writing, yelling at her Keurig for being too slow with the single brew, and doing anything but writing in her favorite writing groups, *Fiction Writing*, and *Writing Without Drama* on Facebook.

Andrew Gottlieb
The Ugly Ornament

We always let our daughter, Abby, hang the ugly ornament on the Christmas tree.

The first time my mother saw the ugly ornament, she grabbed me and asked, "What *is* that?"

The ugly ornament is different every year. The first one was Abby's creation, a mass of dust bunnies she'd collected from around the house. In it, I could make out a half-piece of popcorn and a couple of dead flies. We looped some red thread around the mass, and we hung it on the tree. "Go wash your hands," I'd said.

My mother visits us for Christmas every year, traveling miles across the country. She's vibrant and independent, bossing life as if she'll have the job forever. Her hair is dyed blonde and her wrists clatter with bracelets.

We've had all kinds of things for the ugly ornament. A mass of old bandages from when Abby skinned her knee. A plastic cup filled with dirt. A small collection of dried bird bones. Some charred wooden bits from when Abby's friend Lee's house burned down. Sawdust, spider webs, plastic litter from the beach, rusty cans. A cup of baby teeth. You name it; it's been on the tree.

The ugly ornament doesn't smell. It's the one rule. It's in the house, after all. No poop, nothing rotting. Abby insists that poop and rot should be one of the ornaments, but she understands about the smell. Children can be good at compromising.

My father died years ago, but my mother will never remarry. She's too busy with charities and clubs and tennis to want to negotiate her time again. I understand. In a way, all adults get like this.

That first time she saw the ugly ornament, I explained, "The ugly ornament is so we remember that no matter how wonderful things are, there's pain in the world."

She frowned. "Don't you get enough of that on the news? Christmas is a time for beauty and celebration, dear."

"I know, but not everyone in the world can share in that."

"They're not supposed to share it. It's a family celebration. Beauty. Joy. The birth of Christ, for God's sake."

"There's suffering and pain, too."

"Of course. But not here," she insisted. "Not right now."

I had a flash of inspiration. I said, "I agree with you, but it was Abby's idea."

When I said that, she softened. I could see her struggling with it. After all, she's the one who each year likes to take photos of the tree, surrounded by presents, twinkling with light, covered in the appropriate trappings. But she loves Abby. She understands children.

"I don't know," she said. "Might as well have Christmas at a homeless shelter."

The next year, at the homeless shelter, Abby really got into it, serving food in large helpings. She was very gentle with people, even the ones who had trouble communicating. I made sure there was one small, inexpensive present for everyone, anyone. We bought the tree for the shelter, the largest they'd ever had, and we decorated it with our home ornaments, except without an ugly ornament. The ugly ornament stayed at home, on our small, family tree. We'd debated. My wife suggested a large, dead beetle we found in the garage.

Abby looked at the bug's shiny, green back and said, "That's not ugly. That's beautiful." We settled on a small piece of sod with brown, withered grass and a bent feather stuck in it.

At the shelter, my mother wasn't sure what to do at first. She was dressed nicely, in reds and greens, looking proper as she does, standing to the side, gauging things.

Then the staff approached her, one at a time, thanking her profusely just for being there.

I moved heavy, hot trays of food from the kitchen to the warmers. My wife made sure cutlery got replaced. That napkins were available. There was no end to small chores. Lunch wasn't even over before my mother was circling the room, hugging every single person, greeting them, saying hello, wishing them Happy Christmas, Happy Holidays, holding their hands.

Some people wanted a second hug from her. Except for one person, an older, bearded man who didn't want to be touched. For him, she brought huge, second servings of turkey and stuffing, covered in gravy and with extra cranberry sauce on a separate dish with a clean spoon; and she left it to the side of him, just as he'd requested.

Andrew C. Gottlieb lives and writes in Irvine, California. His work has appeared in *American Fiction, Best New Poets, Denver Quarterly, Ecotone, The Fly Fish Journal, Mississippi Review, Orion,* and *Poetry Northwest.* His new poetry chapbook, *Flow Variations*, is published by Finishing Line Press (December 2017).

Say hello at: www.andrewcgottlieb.com.

Christine Rodriguez
Up in Smoke

I grabbed the partial pack of Kool Lights from the nightstand. There was ash covering everything in the room. Mom had smoked many brands of cigarettes since she started at age 13. She had only used this one for a year. Her way of getting healthy, or so she claimed.

"Don't forget the lighter," my sister, Deb, reminded.

"It's not here." I huffed in frustration. Then a glint caught my eye. "Found it!"

Figures. Under Mom's pillow. We've told her a million times not to smoke in bed. She could start a fire.

Deb grabbed the lighter from my hand. She turned and stared at the familiar object. "Who gave this to her anyway," she asked. "What's so important about this particular lighter?" The expensive silver case sported an intricate etching. A polished red coral sat in the center. The cheap Bic inside seemed unfitting. "Nice," she muttered.

"I don't know." I shrugged. "She's had it for years. Bought it for herself?"

I took it from Deb and rubbed my fingers over the shiny casing where some of the etchings were worn smooth. Mom had a tendency to stroke the surface with her thumb whenever she was nervous. My sensitive nose wrinkled at the sweet smell of lighter fluid. I never took up the habit.

"Maybe it's not so important in itself," I speculated. "It's just what she held in her hands for most of her life, like a security blanket. Have you ever seen her without a cigarette?"

"Guess not," Deb conceded. "We better get them over to her. You know she never leaves this house without them, not even in an emergency."

"Yeah. Unfortunately."

I didn't understand my mother's explicit instructions to put the cigarettes in her left pocket and the lighter in her right. I picked up the well-worn jeans and stashed the objects as per Mom's request. Next, I grabbed the red t-shirt screenprinted with her restaurant logo, SMOKEY JO'S BBQ. Mom was so proud of her creative cuisine. It was a unique and highly successful business and had fast become a household name in our small community.

Smokey Jo's was a favorite hangout of the high school kids. Mom was happy to feed them all, even the ones with little or no money.

The hungry teens were more than happy to sample and review her newest additions to the menu.

Deb grabbed the greasy sneakers and we headed out the door with our mother's standard uniform for work.

A few minutes later we pulled up in front of a Colonial-style building. I looked at Deb, both reluctant to leave the comfort of the heated car. Cheery daffodils bloomed in front of the Garden Creek Funeral Home. I fingered the lighter once more before returning it to the jeans front pocket.

"Lung cancer for crying out loud. And this is what she wants to be cremated with." I shook my head in disbelief. "It's what she wanted. To the very end. She's going for one last smoke but wants her own pack of cigarettes and lighter!"

Chris Rodriguez has retired from conventional life. She currently enjoys gardening and raising backyard chickens at her cottage in Pocatello, Idaho. Her eclectic scribblings have recently appeared in *Rhetoric Askew Anthologies*, *Kelly Jacobson's Anthology of Food-Related Romance*, and a handful of *Thirteen O'Clock Press Anthologies*.

Learn more at: chrisrodriguez-onthebrink.com.

Mary Mullen
Glass Slippers

ydia Pitt had an evil stepmother. Everyone knew. Lydia was much smaller and mousier than her step-brother Peter Dakonovich, who was popular and athletic and dated all the girls. It was unfortunate that they were so close in age and attended the same high school, because no one would have wanted to be compared to Peter. Lydia's brown bangs were too long and hung in her eyes and her hair was always greasy, but Peter's never was, so you knew there was a shower at home. It's not like with Daisy Miller—who didn't have a shower at home, only an old rusted out tub, that we all agreed we wouldn't get in either.

We knew Lydia Pitt's stepmother was evil because we had been to her birthday party the year her father and Peter's mother got married and they had a new house that everyone wanted to see. Lydia's stepmother had found blood on the inside of Lydia's white jeans buried at the bottom of the laundry pile and walked all over the house waving them around telling everyone that Lydia had ruined her jeans.

"Didn't your mother teach you anything? No, of course, she didn't."

It couldn't have been more awkward.

Lucky for Lydia, there weren't that many people there to begin with. Peter was standing in the kitchen with his finger down his throat pretending to puke, while we all stared down at the creamy linoleum, waiting for the pizza to arrive.

Lydia Pitt could have gotten contacts, she could have taken a shower after gym class, she could have taken a scissors to those bangs. She could have talked to someone, anyone, instead of keeping her head down. But she didn't. And we watched her because of it.

And we watched Allen Polbey too—mostly because at 221 pounds he was the largest ninth grader in the school and was kind of hard to miss. So, Allen's actions and inactions and interactions were noted by all of us, because he had been picked on relentlessly until he was so big no one dared, and we all wondered if some day he would exact his revenge on his tormenters. But it turned out he wasn't very vengeful. In fact, he seemed to be more of a lover than a fighter. Which was confirmed on the day we watched Allen Polbey present poor greasy Lydia Pitt with a pair of tiny glass slippers. He presented them to her in the hallway, in front of her locker, amidst a swell of pushing and shoving and metal lockers slamming. We stood on our toes to see past those kids, watching them breathlessly between bells. The aquamarine glass sat swaddled in his chubby fat hand, and we overheard him say, "Here I thought you might like these."

None of us could think of why anyone would need a pair of tiny glass sippers, or why a fifteen-year-old would want something so childish, or where in the world Allen Polbey would have found them. We really couldn't fathom how unlikely a pair the greasy girl and the giant might make. But when she reached to pick them up, she was smiling, and when we heard the bell ring, none of us looked away, because for a fleeting second, she kind of looked like a princess and he kind of looked like a prince.

Mary Mullen is a writer and policy analyst living in Minneapolis, Minnesota. She was a finalist for the 2016 Indian Review Half K Prize, and her short essays have recently appeared in *Entropy* and *Storm Cellar*.

Learn more at: marydenisemarch.wordpress.com.

Onion Festival Pals © P. Decker

Paul Deblinger

Kafka's Team

hen I lived in Prague, I visited the Director of Prague's Jewish Community in the Jewish Town Hall. He had an office on the third floor of the 14th-century building just across from the Old-New Synagogue, the *Altenschul*, the oldest synagogue in Europe. Trekking up the stairs to the third floor I could see directly across to a tiny window in the attic of the synagogue. I admit, as one not attuned to mysticism, that the attic seemed to hold an ethereal glow—in legend it was the place that held the Golem, a man fashioned of clay by Rabbi Loew ben Bezalel, The Maharal of Prague, in the 16th century. Legend says the giant clay man would come alive when the Rebbe placed a prayer in his clay mouth. When he came alive, by his enormous size alone, he was a force for protecting the Jews of Prague. It is said the clay man still lies in repose in the attic awaiting The Maharal's prayer.

I sat down in an old upholstered chair, the loose fabric buttons poking me, and surveyed the office walls. They were covered with certificates, flyspecked photographs, and prints of Josefov, Prague's Jewish Quarter. A photograph in the center of the wall directly over the Director's chair grabbed my eye. It was a creased, old photo of a baseball team. I could barely make out the script on the front of the jerseys; it looked like it read "Abraham." One player, clearly taller than the others, dominated the old photo.

The Director came in and we exchanged pleasant salutations. He saw my eyes wander over his head and turned to see what I was looking at. In his heavy Czech accent, he said, "You like baseball photograph, ah!"

He moved a plant, took the photo off the wall, handed it to me. "This was before my time," he said, "but some men here remember. See small man on end, first row?" He tapped his index finger on the man's head.

I looked at the man, maybe five foot five, scrawny.

"Who is that?" I asked.

"You know writer, Kafka? That's him," he said.

"Kafka played baseball?"

"Kafka loved baseball. His friend who emigrated to America at the turn of century, came back and what he brought back was baseball." He continued, "Kafka immediately took an interest in baseball—its pastoral beauty, pace of game not governed by clock, even fair adjudication by umpires."

He leaned back in his chair. I leaned forward, impatient for more.

One spring Kafka got urge to play. He played catch with Cantor Ezra and played in some practices. He wasn't bad. Kafka's friend Shlomo, manager of team, an accountant for insurance company where Kafka worked, liked him, put him on team.

There was Czech league, eight teams all over Bohemia and Moravia. Abraham team travelled, winning slightly more than they lost, but they were missing one element that would guarantee them championship: strong pitcher.

Toward end of season, Abrahams were in running for championship and had home games against rest of league. Kafka and Shlomo talked about their situation one night over beer at a pub near Old-New Synagogue. He convinced Kafka to talk to Rabbi Zev.

Kafka and Rabbi Zev had regular meeting every Tuesday night at restaurant directly across from Old-New Synagogue. They talked Jewish law, proverbs, philosophy. That night Kafka posed an unusual question for him: "How can Abraham team win league title?"

Rabbi Zev put his head in his hands, in deep thought. He suddenly lifted his head, stood up, turned around, pointed to very top of Altenschul.

The next day as Rabbi Zev instructed, Kafka waited outside ballpark in dark corner behind right field. He showed up exactly on time, with a gentleman that Kafka immediately thought was biggest man he ever saw. Giant, in fact.

Rabbi Zev walked toward Kafka leaving big man behind. He leaned and whispered into Kafka's ear. "He is strong, very strong. He has wicked fast pitch."

The Director pointed to the names in small type at the bottom of the old photograph, handing me a small magnifying glass, again tapping his finger on the head of the tall man standing in the top row, third from the left. The third from the left name on the bottom read: *David Golem.*

The Director's eyes narrowed, his lips closed. Under his breath, he said as if in prayer, "Kafka's team won league that year, won championship!"

Paul Deblinger has an M.A. in English and Creative Writing from Hollins College and an M.F.A. in Creative Writing from Bowling Green State University. He has published in the *Hampden-Sydney Review, Poetry Now, The Black Warrior Review, Cargoes, Window, Minnesota Monthly, The Blood-Horse, Hoofbeats* and others.

Gita Smith

Roadside Attraction

Breau blew in after midnight, stinking under the arms and covered in clay. He'd rolled the four-wheeler in a ditch—to avoid hitting a deer, he *said*. More likely he'd fallen asleep drunk and woke up in six inches of filthy water. I told him to whoa right there in the laundry room and strip. He showered with his ball cap still on, gripping the shower nozzle with one hand and soaping his body with the other.

Breau liked the red wine, creature comforts, boiled shrimp and moonlight on the bayou, in that order. He loved his babies and me, and he always came home, no matter how late or how flavored his blood was with alcohol. When the circuit judge of Feliciana Parish took away his driver's license for the final time, Breau just bought a Yamaha 4-wheeler and drove off-road between home and Ti-Louis' roadhouse and the lumber yard left to him by his drunk of a Daddy.

When he flipped the Yamaha the first time, I took the key away until he had roll bars installed. The second time, I rounded up the children and had them beg Breau to wear a helmet. He started to cry midway through the intervention. But he never did trade his ball cap for protection.

The women in my family have a talent for marrying mannish boys. We like them tall and strong, but we never check under the hood to see if they're fully grown. You can love a man till death do you part, but never marry a shrimper, a drunk, or a preacher. You don't want to be the wife of anyone who wears white boots or kills himself young or tells other people they're going to hell. No good can come of it.

So Breau had flipped the quad for the third time. The next morning while he was sleeping it off, I borrowed a truck with a winch to find the crash site. I took our eldest, Jorge, along in case there was a chance we could right the vehicle and ride it home. What we found was a flattened mess of metal and ABS plastic, its roll bar reduced to tinsel by the force of the impact when the quad landed, top down. Me, I'm no believer, but the fact that Breau was alive is theological proof of the miraculous. Jorge stared at the tangled remains in the ditch for several long minutes, his hands thrust into his jeans back pockets, his thin young face a question mark.

"We gonna leave this here?" he asked.

"Best to. We gonna let your Daddy come look at it."

"What if someone takes it away? For scrap?" Jorge asked.

"Let's put a note on it," I said. "Write, EVIDENCE. DO NOT TOUCH."

That evening, at sunset, I drove Breau down to see the 4-wheeler. He was clear-headed after a long sleep and a meal. There is a certain stage of sobriety among men who drink every night when they are their best selves— reasonable and generous with affection. During these few hours, they can accomplish great things. They write chapters of their novels, fix cars, raise their young ones. They also make promises. Oh, how they make promises.

Breau approached the remains of his off-road sport utility vehicle. He stood some distance away, at first, edgy as if it was a sow who might charge him for approaching her shoats. Then he took slow, careful steps, stopping again 10 feet from the ditch.

"It ain't a snake, Breau," I said. "It won't rear up and bite you."

His legs were shaking. He brought his hands up to his face and sank down on his knees in the damp red clay.

"Oh God, Oh SHIT!" he wailed. "How did this happen? Why don't I remember this happenin'?"

"You were drunk, plain and simple," I said.

There's no point in beating a man when he's down,

and there's no point in acting the wine sheriff. All those women in my family who married callow men, they sure did try though. But none of their nagging made a whit of difference. You can't save someone from himself.

But a man who sees the miraculous in his own life and who sees his mortality cartwheeling away at the side of a two-lane blacktop road—that's a man who just *might* stand a chance. Not of being saved, but of saving himself.

It could happen.

Gita M. Smith is a former reporter for *The Atlanta Journal-Constitution* and the *Montgomery Advertiser*. She's a founding member of the international flash fiction group, House of Writers. When she is not writing, she reads submissions for *Easy Street* and hosts readings of new work by Alabama writers.

Gregg Cusick
Calling

*I*s it ringing, is it ringing?

The two of them, Shani and Fiona, good Catholic girls from County Mayo, in their best dresses, squeezed into the telephone box.

Fiona holds the receiver because it is her beau, Quinn, on the other end. Shani, best friend and keeper of all secrets, is the lookout.

"We're right aside St. Mary's for heaven's sake," Fiona whisper-giggles into the phone. "I can read the hours of confession on the sign from here!" But then she seems overcome by her girlishness and falls silent. Quinn might've asked what is it, or are you still there? Fiona says, "Say something, anything, I just want to hear your voice, not mine."

She looks to Shani whose face shows disapproval perhaps, or some disappointment. Fiona doesn't know, can't read if she's said too much or too little, or just something silly or over-emotional. But Quinn must've taken her words alright, because there is a quiet pause for a moment then the sound of his voice, the smooth blending of his words strung together sounding to Shani like a steady rain, a comforting steady shower pattering on rooftops. And Fiona does seem comforted, even more, near enraptured and Shani feels an energy, its smell something she knows and can hardly grasp, let alone name. Shani feels an excitement, and envy.

They had been to the dance that night at St. Mary's, a stilted smoky affair in the downstairs meeting room where the high windows looked out over the cemetery. The dead Catholics looked on with disapproval as a courageous pair might get too close on the dance floor, and the good Sister Claire would have to step in, like a referee at a prizefight for heaven's sake, to make sure the sixteen-year-old boys and girls kept their distance. But mostly it was boys on the street-side—plenty of distance—while the girls huddled and giggled and blushed on the cemetery-side of the hall. Shani was happiest here beside Fiona, touching her arm or hand, even adjusting her hair, like a lover, she thought to herself. And that Fiona showed no interest in the Catholic boys gave her hope still, that she could confess someday what she wanted, what she felt for Fiona, hope that this affection might be returned.

But leaving the dance, Fiona had gripped her arm and looked near-loving into Shani's expectant, not daring to expect, hopeful face, and asked, "Would you come with me to the booth I'm going to call Quinn."

Shani's disappointment broke suddenly, a dark wave over her face, and she looked down and breathed in and looked back up.

"What is it?"

"I'm just afraid for you and Quinn. But of course I'll go with you."

And they stepped out of the misting night into the booth, Shani trying to be satisfied, falling drunk so close to Fiona she could smell the lilac perfume and cigarettes from her breath and coat. She wished the moment never to end. Is it ringing? She leaned closer still, until she heard Quinn's smooth expectant voice.

Gregg Cusick's short story collection, *My Father Moves Through Time Like a Dirigible*, was published by Livingston Press in 2014. He lives in Durham, North Carolina, where he bartends and tutors literacy.

Ashley Memory
Lost and Found of the Dead

*E*very city had one, and it was usually tucked away in the far corners of a decrepit office building. In Raleigh, according to the clerk who grudgingly looked up the address, it was in the basement of 92 West Main, the same building where people paid their parking tickets and filed their complaints. The hours are irregular, she warned, because the custodian was an old man who should have retired years ago.

"Nobody else would have that job," she muttered, "so the people in charge let him do what he wants."

There wasn't a sign but when I entered Suite 05A, I knew I was in the right place. The custodian, a man with long graying hair tied in a ponytail, greeted me with the curtest of nods. My long-festering curiosity had driven me there, so I stood my ground, waited for his attention.

"How can I help you?" he finally said.

"So where do you keep all those priceless jewels?" I asked, trying to be funny. "Maybe a lost Rembrandt or two?"

He grimaced, and I felt stupid because I realized he must hear this all the time.

"Those things would be upstairs," he said, "in the Unclaimed Property Department." He plopped down on a rolling stool while he jammed his glasses up the length of his nose. "Let me show you what I do have."

With a surprising energy, he opened drawer after drawer. They were divided by category, each one marked with a hand-lettered label. At a glance I could see drawers for "Second Thoughts," "Broken Promises," and "Pointless Arguments."

"There's no paper, of course," he said, as though he had read my mind. "No one writes anymore."

But the words were there. I leaned into the drawer for "Unrequited Love." It was dark inside, but the drawer was full. It overflowed with melancholy, a slur of notes ending on a low whistle, like the song of a bird who has lost its mate. And it went on and on and on.

The custodian grunted as he slammed each drawer shut. "Here's what nobody can believe," he said, rolling over to the other side of the room. He opened the middle drawer of a cabinet that spanned the entire wall. And although he didn't say so, I knew I was staring into "Apologies." This drawer was the loudest, and it sounded like a million little murmurs that blended into one monotonous buzz. Hearing it made my head ache.

I immediately thought of my own regrets. A daisy chain of the times when I should have apologized but never did. To a co-worker for a snide remark during a meeting, to my mother for bowing out of Sunday's dinner, and to the driver of the white Hyundai I cut off on the interstate this morning. Then I thought of Dan, my fiancé, and the many arguments that just frittered away without me taking my share of the blame. How long would we go on?

"What people don't realize," the custodian said quietly as if talking to himself, "is that apologies don't cost a damn thing."

My face blushed hot with shame.

Fortunately, he sensed my uneasiness. He averted his eyes and cleared his throat. I noticed the sandwich on his desk.

"I'm sorry," he said, "but it's time for my lunch and I have to lock up now. You can come back at 2 if . . ."

"No, no," I said, having seen quite enough. I thanked him for his time and escaped into the hall. The door behind me closed like a vault.

Outside, the sun shone brighter than before; the meteorologist, who had predicted rain, was wrong. Everyone around me, the man walking his schnauzer, the young pony-tailed mother pushing a stroller of twins, and even the ordinarily grim-faced crossing guard at the corner of Main and Church seemed unusually happy.

I thought of humming a light tune but nothing came to mind. So I walked as fast as I could, never glancing back at 92 West Main. I wanted to be happy too.

I fumbled inside my purse for my cell phone. Then I called Dan, to hear his voice, to make things right between us.

"Hi," he said. "Everything okay?"

"Long story," I said. "Let's talk tonight."

Ashley Memory writes fiction, essays, and poetry. Her work has appeared in *The Thomas Wolfe Review, Wildlife in North Carolina, Romantic Homes, Brilliant Flash Fiction, The Naugatuck Review,* and *The Gyroscope Review.* Her work is forthcoming in the annual baseball review, *The Hardball Times.*

Read more from Ashley on her blog: ashley-memory.com/naked-and-hungry.

Standard Diner © Angela Kubinec

Mary Mullen
Another Night at the 9-1 Supper Club

Alma Hixton had been going to the 9-1 Supper Club for 49 years. And because Garrett had always insisted they go on Friday evening, she would always curl her hair on Friday afternoons, when the sun was high and the marigolds on the back patio browned at the edges in the dry western heat, just as she had done today. She came in quietly and took her seat by the front window, not too far from the door. She could see Jeanie filling the ketchup bottles in the back. She knew she would come over soon and say, "How are you doing, honey?" She knew, because that is what people all over town had been saying all week.

Growing up on her father's alfalfa farm there had been few occasions to dine out. No one in her family took part in the kind of socializing that went on at the 9-1 Supper Club—the kind of socializing that started when good Christians were at home putting their children to bed. She remembers that at 19, when Garrett Hussman asked her to go to dinner with him, came to pick her up in his light blue Ford, she looked back at her parents standing in the doorway and wondered if her mother had ever left the house after dark. She honestly hadn't thought about what it might be like to be waited on, to have her water cup filled, to have the napkins laundered, to have Angela Lentz's mother scurry around the linoleum-tiled dining room to get her a saucer of Beefsteak Sauce, since these were only ever things she had done at home, where she had been the one scurrying.

The first night he picked her up, Garrett had on a denim collared shirt, which was different than the other men, whose white dress shirts looked crisp and uncomfortable, but after he took off his cowboy hat and gave a handshake and hello to every table—leaving Alma alone to look over the menu, to feel the inside of her knees get wet and sticky against the vinyl booth—she gathered that Garrett was at home here and that if she was with him, she would be too.

He took her out the next Friday, and the one after. In the years that followed, she would miss it only for childbirth, pneumonia, and the annual Omaha Corn Expo. She would lament the removal of the country fried steak so noisily that Arnold's son Peter would put it back on the menu. She would grumble when the ham soup stopped tasting like the ham soup she knew, and louder still, when it disappeared altogether.

But Garrett never minded, he would try each new special, flirt with each new young waitress, lament each of their ultimate departures—but always with a handshake, always wishing them well.

She looked down at the menu, even though she knew exactly what was on it, even though she knew she would order the hot turkey dinner again tonight. It's off-putting, she thought, that the late afternoon sun is still so bright at supper time, that the front windows are left uncovered, that the tile floor is faded, that the tint of the table is muted by years in the western sun. Had she never noticed the nails coming loose from the wood frames on the doorway? The deep cracks in the asphalt in the nearly empty parking lot? Then she looked across the table to where Garrett had always sat and noticed that there was a tear in the back of the booth that she had never seen. He must have sat against it all those years. And then she wondered about what she would do, while she waited for her dinner, wondered how she could possibly stay, without him there to talk to.

Mary Mullen is a writer and policy analyst living in Minneapolis, Minnesota. She was a finalist for the 2016 Indian Review Half K Prize, and her short essays have recently appeared in *Entropy* and *Storm Cellar*.

Learn more at: marydenisemarch.wordpress.com.

Michelle Donice

Mrs. Beasley and the Witching Hour

Mama called the hour between 3:00 and 4:00 a.m. the witching hour. She said that's when she got her mojo. Night after night, during that hour, I would awaken with a start wiping away dream images of full moons and moss burdened trees from my sleep-encrusted eyes.

In my dream, the witches never spoke, but their gnarled fingers reached for me. Toothless mouths stretched like forgotten caves in dark faces. The deep lines around their black eyes were the topography which frightened me most. Their desire for me sent me running barefoot down the hallway to Mama's closed bedroom door. Barely taller than the handle, I turned it and tried to push the door open but it never budged.

Through the closed door I whispered: "Mama, the witches tried to get me."

There would be movement, muffled voices and either a man's nervous laughter or a cough before the lights flickered on. Then my mama's voice: "Go back to bed. Dreams aren't real."

But I knew that wasn't true. I would stand for a moment, in the darkness outside her door, hoping she would walk me back to bed, but she never did.

Once back in my bedroom I was terrified because the witches would be waiting. I pulled the pink bedspread over my head and tried to fight off sleep. Eventually I returned to their grotesque world of drums and smoke. In the twilight between the world that existed in our small house and the world where the witches waited, there was always unfriendly laughter. I was never sure if it was Mama's, the witches, or one of the uncles.

By morning, they were gone—careful not to leave any trace behind. I lay listening for their cackle and the rhythm of the drums but they had evaporated like dew in the morning sun. It was the uncles I heard instead. Some made Mama giggle as they tiptoed toward the front door and others made her curse as she bolted the lock behind them. I never learned to distinguish the witches one from another, but I learned to tell the uncles apart by the names she called them.

The uncles who wanted to come again would bring gifts for her and sometimes for me. She always set the gift next to a bowl of cereal before retreating to the patio with cigarettes and the telephone. On this morning, I could hear snippets of her conversation as I ate. Her beautiful manicured feet rested against the railing and, occasionally, she flicked ashes into the ceramic bowl I made for her at summer camp. It was not supposed to be an ashtray.

Once before, an uncle left a Mickey Mouse watch and I spent all day watching the big, gloved hands move around the dial. I could not tell time, but I was fascinated. Another uncle brought Twister and I played alone on the floor as Mama went into her room with a different uncle.

On this morning, there was a box with a doll inside. It was nothing like my Baby Alive with soft skin and a smiling mouth that took a bottle. This doll was old with large blue eyes peering from behind wire-rimmed glasses. Her hair was short and blonde and she wore a blue and white polka-dot dress.

I opened the patio door and waited for Mama to notice me. I held out the doll, but she kept talking on the phone.

"Girl, he got her that creepy ass Mrs. Beasley doll from Family Affair! Said he found it online."

I could hear laughter through the phone.

I took the doll back inside confused about what was so funny. I tried to finish my cereal, but it was soggy.

Mama said, "Girl, no…hell no, he wants children. I don't even want the one I have."

I froze; the spoon halfway to my mouth.

That night I pulled back the covers and climbed into bed with Mrs. Beasley. The shadows danced on the walls when the witches came for me cloaked in darkness, a full moon suspended in a dreamscape sky. I watched them move to the rhythm of disembodied drums. Hunchbacked and withered-faced, they stared from behind trees; their gnarled fingers reaching for me.

This time, I reached back.

Michelle Donice is an MFA Student at Sierra Nevada College. She lives in Nashville, Tennessee and teaches composition and Creative Writing courses. She has written one novel, *The Other Side of Through,* and enjoys hiking, yoga, playing Scrabble, and spending time with her dog, Simba.

Visit her website at www.michelledonice.com.

Michael Oberly
A Saturday Service

C uyler and Grimm cut it to a one-run game in the bottom of the third. I am the only person in the bleachers not cheering. The Yankees go 1-2-3 in the top of the fourth. The Cubs tie it up when Lazzeri boots a grounder in the bottom of the fourth. The fifth inning starts, and Tully hasn't shown. *Fired?* Certainly. *Arrested?* Very likely. *With me?* Hardly.

Ruth emerges from the dugout to a cloudburst of hatred. He is alone but strong: I had never realized how he could have passed for Tully's dad. He tiptoes to the plate and raises his giant bat—not at Charlie Root or the Cubs bench or even the fifty thousand screaming throats —at *me*. Faithless, he accuses, his bat unwavering. Faithless and undeserving.

Break hot daylight on your blushing neck as you break from the shadows.

That summer of '32 Babe Ruth hit 41 home runs, only eleven less than the Cubs' starters hit *combined*. This was normally the kind of thing I'd rub in Tully's face, but since his beloved idiots overcame their inborn mediocrity and won the pennant in September, my gloating had to wait. Not long, though, since the Yankees took the first two games of the Series handily in New York and then got on the 20th Century to Chicago.

The path of least resistance dictates your pace but not your direction past the well-dressed jerks who can afford their tickets.

Tully's ma was as pretty as her son was ugly; that's why he got the job. Mr. Dietrich, the Wrigley concession manager, "had eye" for Tully's ma. ("Eye", singular: the other one was hand-painted on a chipped tin mask that covered half his face). Dietrich had pulled some strings to get Tully hired in mid-August for five bucks a game—great money for a twelve-year-old and a damn sight better than the ten cents a frame I made setting pins at Merle's. What Tully's ma did with that money Tully sure as hell didn't say, so I didn't know.

"Thief!" someone screams as you pound past them towards the head of the line—Tully's line.

What I *did* know was that Tully was uptight as hell about the job, paranoid he was going to screw up and lose it. Any thoughts of him being a "soft touch" bounced off the curb almost as hard as the one and only kid who'd tried hopping Tully's turnstile.

Knees high, eyes wide—a tin mask appears at Tully's shoulder.

"The organ there s-sounds like ch-church," Tully would say when he was feeling particularly soupy. I knew only too well what a church organ sounded like—Wrigley's didn't sound a damn bit similar. "Y-you have R-Ruth, I have Wr-wrigley."

Tully cleverly hid his stutter by never talking to anyone but me. Terrible taste in teams aside, he was just about the only guy I knew who loved baseball more than me and that fall, what with my mom and all, I was only too happy to lose myself with him. I looked out for him though he was big as an ox.

Long muscles in your thighs sing the melody, short muscles in your calves the harmony.

"M-maybe don't be a Y-Yankees fan," Tully told me the first day of school. I was nursing a bloody lip and bloodier knuckles from the North Side trogs who'd tried to take my signed cap.

"Maybe stop breathing?" I had retorted.

Tully's meaty arm rises up reflexively as you leap—his eyes have met yours.

"D-Dietrich's g-going to ask M-Ma to m-marry him tomorrow," Tully had said. Maybe he'd been crying.

Tully's fist connects but not with you—the tin mask joins you in flight—a gasp from the crowd. You land close enough to Mr. Dietrich to hear his sobbing, then roll to your feet and dash off into the cowardly alone with hardly a backward glance.

Hardly.

When Ruth raises his bat again it is to bludgeon Root's next pitch.

When they scream and clamber atop one another. I let myself be swept along.

When reflex alone reaches out my bare hand, I welcome only its hot sting.

His dainty trot brings me no solace; throwing back his ball no relief.

The organist plays a happy tune. The service goes on and on.

Mike Oberly is determined to use the MFA in Creative Writing he earned from Western New England University as recklessly and irresponsibly as possible. He lives in Western Massachusetts with his wife and daughter.

Grow Old Along With Me © Nena A. Callaghan

Linda C. Wisniewski
Dinner for Five

The dark red Chrysler minivan pulled into the crowded school parking lot and glided slowly into a space between two cars. A tall, slender woman with swinging brown hair opened the driver's side door and stepped out. Her navy slacks and blazer were slightly wrinkled. She marched with stiff, sure steps to the spot where a couple in their sixties stood on the sidewalk.

The man wore an unzipped jacket, khaki pants and comfortable looking brown shoes. The woman had dressed that morning in a pink jogging suit and white running shoes. They each held the hand of a small child. Their feet were poised and still, between coming and going, leaving and staying.

"There's been a change of plans." The younger woman's voice cracked the silence. She stepped forward and took a child's hand in each of her own, gently but firmly forcing them to let go of the older couple.

The small boy and girl looked up at the woman, eyes wide and mouths open. Their matching blue and red backpacks dragged on the ground as the woman steadily pulled them away. The boy looked back at the older couple. His buzz cut was so short his scalp was visible. As he moved away, the back of his head with his ears sticking out on the sides looked so vulnerable, the older man thought of buying him a baseball hat to give him some protection.

"We love you," the man said.

His words stirred the woman at his side. "Yes, we love you."

The children did not hear. Already in the van, they buckled their seatbelts. The man put his arm around her shoulders and slowly turned her away from them, before the loud heavy door of the Chrysler slid along its track and closed with a clunk.

The couple walked to their light gray Honda. He opened the passenger door and waited until she got inside before closing it with a quiet final click.

"I suppose," said his wife when he had settled behind the wheel, "we should call Tom."

The man turned the key in the ignition. "I don't know. It's hard to know what to do. We don't want to mess up his custody hearing."

He drove slowly through the school parking lot to the exit. The Chrysler minivan had stopped in front of them, waiting for traffic on the road to clear. He imagined the children waving out the back window, smiling, but he could not see them. All the van's windows were tinted to keep out the light.

That night, the couple's house seemed quieter than usual. "Let's go to Applebee's," the man said.

"Yes, let's," his wife answered. "I still have that gift card from the insurance company." She picked up her sweater and followed her husband out the door.

It was dark when they got to the restaurant parking lot. The tall bright lights on poles made all the cars shine.

"Is that their van?" she asked, peering out the windshield.

"Hmmm. Could be. But lots of people have vans like that."

"Let's go inside."

The hostess walked them to a booth far away from the bar, in a cozy corner near a window.

"Grandma! Grandpa!" Two children ran to hug their knees, almost knocking them off balance. The older woman grabbed onto the back of the booth, laughing.

"Hey, hey, let's not knock them over!" The woman looked embarrassed, but she nodded at the couple. "Sorry we were in a hurry before, at the school."

"No problem!" The grandfather said. "Say, would you

care to join us?"

She looked down at her hands.

"Say yes, Momma, say yes!" the little girl pleaded, jumping up and down.

The little boy just hung his head and held on to his grandfather's hand.

The mother saw the look on the grandparents' faces as they tried to be friendly and not too hopeful. As if they were afraid she might say no. The older woman reminded her of her Grandma who had loved her all her life. What had she been thinking? What kind of person was she, to take her children away from their only grandparents? Whatever happened with her marriage, these people were not at fault. They loved her kids, too, she knew that. And they had never done anything to harm her. She smiled at the couple, nodded her head and turned to the hostess.

"We'll be five," she said.

Linda C. Wisniewski lives with her retired scientist husband in Bucks County, PA. She writes for a weekly newspaper, teaches memoir workshops and has been published in the *Christian Science Monitor* and the *Philadelphia Inquirer*. Linda's memoir, *Off Kilter*, was published in 2008 by Pearlsong Press.

She blogs at www.lindawis.com/blog.

Chris Coulson
Enough is Enough is Good Enough

I was shopping at Home Depot and there was Granddad in the Garden Center. I was buying bags of bark for my garden when I saw him. I was on the other side of one of those long tall shelves, so I hid and watched him through the hole I made in the stacks of bark bags and wheelbarrows.

No one in the family has seen him for years, nobody talks about him. The last time I saw him he was standing in his front yard, shirt off, holding some shoes and underwear against his chest with a stranger standing between him and his wife, his family and his house, the stranger pointing down the street. The way he wanted Granddad to go. The family had called the stranger to the house to intervene, to "start a dialogue," to "set boundaries." I remember those phrases, and others, being used that day, and didn't care for this kind of dialogue; I wanted to take Granddad and *run for the border*. The stranger was reasonable, calm, and bigger than Granddad.

We, the family, sat at the dining room table while this

man told my Granddad he had to get out of his own home. Granddad wasn't hearing this, he was looking around the room for a bottle of anything, but when he did hear what was being said, he looked at the man and asked, "Who are you again, sir?"

I was the only one at the table who laughed, Granddad smiled over at me and we both laughed. Granddad found his busted eyeglasses on the table, slid them on, and squinted at the stranger.

"Josh is my name, sir. I'm here to facilitate a dialogue between you and your family. They need you to leave until you come to terms with your drinking. Is that cool with you?" Josh put on his sympathetic face, the family put on their sympathetic church faces. Granddad stood up, alone on his side of the room, red-faced, yelling then weeping, only his striped pajama bottoms on, hitting himself again and again in the forehead with his hands, trying to talk but only making sounds between slapping himself and crying.

Over the years, he'd told jokes, made toasts, carved turkeys standing there at the head of the table.

I left. I went out, got in my car, and watched as Granddad, Josh, and the family ran out onto the front lawn, Granddad hugging his clothes, screaming but not really at anyone, getting into his car, and driving away wildly in his pajamas. Josh and the family went back into the house, hugging each other.

Later, Grandma divorced Granddad.

The family moved on with their lives, and all the rest.

Then, that day at Home Depot. Granddad, looking at flowers and little trees. I'd never seen him this patient. He'd pick up a plant, feel the leaves, smell the flower, read the plastic card stuck into the dirt. One flower at a time.

He was humming, had on a tie, long-sleeved shirt rolled up, navy tattoos, hands covered with earth, looking down at some kind of a flower, fascinated, and smiling.

I stopped hiding, pushed my cart nearby.

"What's that one?" I asked.

"Night blooming jasmine," he said, smiling down at it.

"Smells good," I said.

"Yes. Plant it near the bedroom window, you have it in your dreams all night." He looked up; I'd forgotten how blue his eyes were.

"Well. Look who's here."

"Hi, Granddad. Nice tie, by the way."

"Thanks. I like red and blue together. Got it at St. Vincent's." He looked over my shoulder. "Anyone else with you?"

"No, just me."

"You like gardening?"

"Yeah. Peaceful."

"It is. Better late than never. How is everybody?" Granddad asked, gently fingering leaves.

"Oh, you know. Moving on with their lives."

Granddad coughed, or laughed.

"What happened after that day, after you drove away?" I expected him to get the clichéd far-away look in his eyes.

He didn't, he was right there with me.

"Everything." He wasn't joking. "But not anymore. Now, it's not everything all the time. It's just enough, you know?" He laughed. "Is that cryptic enough for you?"

"No, I know what you mean." I laughed, and we hugged each other. "Besides, what's wrong with cryptic?"

"Not a thing. Lunch?"

I said, "Yes."

We left the flowers where they were. They'll always be there for us.

Chris Coulson was a bartender, morgue attendant and obituary writer (simultaneously!), newspaper reporter and actor before writing his first novel, *Nothing Normal in Cork*, followed by his first collection of poetry, *The Midwest Hotel*. His second novel, *Red Jumbo*, will be out in 2018.

Visit Chris at chriscoulson.net.

Jane Shlensky
What is Kept

My husband is sniffing t-shirts, testing the elastic on ancient underpants, stacking old newspapers and magazines, leafing through and rereading articles.

"I forgot about these. This is good stuff!" he shouts from the adjoining room. I refuse to be drawn into his method of decluttering the house, where nothing is disposable and everything is "perfectly good." I say slash and burn, swallow sentimentality and approach belongings with callous energy until almost everything is discarded or repurposed. In this and so much, we are opposites. He says a person never knows when he will need a thing; I say it's time to downsize and open up some space to breathe.

I stare into my over-stuffed closet clogged with hard choices before deciding to tackle the bureau first, tiny drawers full of ticket stubs, single socks, and random broken jewelry—easy decisions.

Until I run across the box.

My dad gave my sister and me pearls for Christmas when we were twelve and fourteen, each double strands in small velvet oyster-shaped cases, hers aqua and mine cranberry. Both were in their original cardboard boxes, unwrapped, with our names on them, no card, no ribbons. Mama did all the shopping and gift-giving in our house; Daddy just signed his name to her efforts. Daddy generally gave money in an envelope, never comfortable giving or wrapping gifts. When it came to Daddy and special occasions, we had lowered our expectations years before, which made the pearls especially delightful. We loved them, wore them, and lost them over the years. Perhaps Greta still has hers squirreled away, but mine are long gone. I don't need the box.

Still what a marvel of a box it is, well made, sturdy, filled now with old passports and drivers' licenses, photos, boarding passes, nothing dear. It's time to toss it and its contents, but I don't. On its lid, Daddy had written my name, Laura, in his best handwriting. I imagine he hovered over the box, wondering what to write, then landed on the simplicity of our names. No "to" or "from," no 'Happy' anything, just our names, Greta and Laura. I imagine he pressed the blue ballpoint into the cardboard, for the L wavers slightly, evidence of his taking pains with his handwriting, careful to make my name beautiful.

My father could barely tolerate the giving of gifts, although he put on a cheerful face when receiving them. We labeled him curmudgeon and let him hand out cash. But this box proves our judgment wrong. Here on this box is evidence that, at least one time, he was mindful, he cared, and he tried, evidence that my father loved us. I hold the box closer to smell it. Empty and refill it. Return its lid lightly brushing my fingertips across the letters. I close my eyes and try to swallow the familiar burn in my throat, memories of my father tangled in me. Then I clear away the clutter, wrap the box in a silk scarf, and return it to the drawer.

Jane Shlensky, veteran teacher and musician, has recent poetry in a number of literary journals and anthologies. The North Carolina Poetry Society nominated her poem, *Insomnia*, for a 2017 Pushcart Prize, their second nomination of her poetry, and three of her short fiction pieces were contest finalists. Jane's chapbook *Barefoot on Gravel* (2016) is available from Finishing Line Press.

Find her online: http://www.writersdigest.com/whats-new/write-poetry-jane-shlensky.

"There are perhaps
no days of our childhood
we lived so fully
as those we spent
with a favorite book."
—Marcel Proust

Take Me Home © Brittany Murdock

Ashley Memory
Saving Cedric

I ced tea tastes best in thin glasses," said Aunt Lillian, shaking her head at the tray of tumblers I had just brought out. "But now that you've poured it, never mind." She flicked her diamond-encrusted fingers toward my mother and me. "You two can drink it. I will go without." Then she looked at me. "I know you've got him."

"Who?" I asked although I knew perfectly well whom she was talking about.

"Cedric," she said. "That godforsaken dog of his."

My cousin Willie had been dead only two days but it felt much, much longer. We had kidnapped Cedric with good reason. Aunt Lillian wanted to have him put to sleep and bury him with her son. For the last two days, the family had been shuttling the little Daschund-Chihuahua mix between our homes. Now the dog was at our house, locked up in the basement, while we waited until his owner was lowered into the ground without him. Cedric was an obnoxious little thing but putting him to sleep was the last thing Willie would have wanted.

"Holly Ann, you may think that if you hide him long enough, it'll be too late," she said, fixing her narrow face and crystal blue eyes at me. She played with the braided trim of her coral velour lounger. "But I don't forget."

Even at twelve years old, I knew that grief sometimes did funny things to people, but Aunt Lillian's insistence on euthanizing her son's dog astounded us all. It was grossly out of proportion with her treatment of Willie while he was alive. I had never heard her utter anything except disdain for her artist son. An undescended testicle had kept him from the distinguished military career that his father had expected, and his cancer diagnosis had come almost as a relief to him. Willie had spent his whole life anticipating his demise. He had shot out one lung in a failed suicide attempt long ago over a girl from Mt. Gilead. All you had to do was to gaze at his mournful portrait of Jesus in the Garden of Gethsemane to know that he would die young. Cedric was my only connection to him.

Inexplicably, Aunt Lillian's rules of decorum remained with me all my life. Chill celery stalks in ice water to refresh them. Always singe the wicks before setting new candles out. Use dental floss to neatly slice coconut cake.

According to a family legend, as a teen back in 1946, she had been the one to lead her siblings out of a Montgomery County Hospital the night before they were to have their tonsils out, an act I had secretly admired. I often imagined her rules for the escape. Take off your shoes. Walk in a single file. As quiet as a mouse, she would have said to her younger brothers and sisters. We can do this.

Lillian had made no secret of her disdain for Cedric but her grief at her son's passing was a complete surprise. We breathed much easier once Willie was in the ground, but we should have known better. The day after the funeral, the hulking form of Lillian's navy blue 1972 Lincoln Continental rose up in our driveway like a prehistoric shark. And there I was, in the front yard, trying to pacify Cedric with a game of tug-of-war. Instinctively, I grabbed the little dog and rolled him up in my T-shirt. Aunt Lillian emerged slowly from the car, stabbing the ground with her cane. Her eyes burned like propane flames.

"I told you I would be back," she said. "I intend to cremate that little rascal and sprinkle his ashes over the carnations. Give him to me."

My whole life lay before me but I just knew that what I did next would forever define me. I turned and ran. Past the security of home, my own backyard, and into the dark, dark woods. I lost a flip-flop in the bramble but I kept running, skipping over rotten logs and poison ivy. Twice I dropped Cedric, but for once he did not run away. Even he seemed to understand that this wasn't the time to cross me.

"We can do this," I told him, as I clutched his little body to my chest. His heart was beating as fast as mine. "We can do this."

Ashley Memory writes fiction, essays, and poetry. Her work has appeared in *The Thomas Wolfe Review, Wildlife in North Carolina, Romantic Homes, Brilliant Flash Fiction, The Naugatuck Review,* and *The Gyroscope Review.* Her work is forthcoming in the annual baseball review, *The Hardball Times.*

Read more on her blog: ashley-memory.com/naked-and-hungry.

Gita Smith
You Only Get One Question

I met her husband in a greasy coffee shop on the run-down side of town—his choice. I suppose he thought the locale fit my role. I had been sleeping with his wife, after all. That made me trash.

He was a middle-aged tugboat carrying 300 pounds on swollen ankles. He'd come with a bad attitude. The husbands always do. They never consider why their wives go looking elsewhere for pleasure. Or maybe they do consider, but the only answer they can sit with is: some bad influence (me) is to blame for their darling Dottie or sweet Sally-Jo going astray.

"Jesus, how old are you anyway?" he asked.

"That's a boring question," I said. "Of all the things you could ask at a time like this, you want a number?"

He dumped five sugar packets into some oily-looking coffee while I marveled at his eyes: they were kidney beans wrapped in dough.

"I mean, if you want to talk numbers, how much do you weigh?" I asked him back. "That could figure into this, you know."

"Listen, you," he snarled. "Who the fuck do you think you are?"

"Sorry pal," I said, "you only get one question here at the Exit Interview Corral. The answer is 22. And now, if you'll excuse me, there's a circuit court clerk waiting for me at the Marriott Courtyard. She bought herself some sexy new underwear online, and it would be rude to keep her waiting. Rude is what cost her husband his bed privileges."

It was true, I thought, steering my Camaro onto the bypass. Marriage has a fatal flaw. I wouldn't go so far as to say familiarity inevitably breeds contempt. But that kind of rude indifference, of taking the wife for granted, can feel like contempt. After years go by with no touching, the little gal feels bad about herself. Then, I come along, tell her she's desirable, tell her things I'm going to *do to* her, feed her need until all she can think about is me. Before she knows it, she's renting motel rooms for us to sneak away. She feels so alive that she's practically vibrating, like a high-school girl right before a date with the town bad boy.

Her fat fuck of a husband who left her untouched for four years while he watched televised football with *Sara Lee* in his lap has no call blaming me.

I was playing World of Warcraft (*Rise of the Zandalari*) the first time my phone rang for an exit interview. Some shitbird of a lawyer found my number behind the visor of his old lady's Lexus and got curious. He demanded a meet-up: Saturday morning, Eastdale Country Club, he'd give up his second nine holes just to see me.

Oooooh, lucky me!

That's the thing, see. The husbands come to the meet all bowed up for a bush-pissing contest between two dogs. But I show up in full androgyny theater: black leather, high-heeled boots, eyeliner, cubic Z earring. The guys get massively confused. Shitbird's eyes almost crossed when he saw me. I could see the words bubble over his head. *Boy? Girl?* He was trying to put his cookies-and-cream Mary-Lou together with me, but he couldn't figure me for the top or the bottom.

I learned something that day: lawyers are no better than anyone else at asking the right first question.

His was, "What the hell was your number doing in my wife's car?"

"She must have put it there."

And then I was gone. I look at it this way. If the guy wants information, if he wants to fix things between him and the wife, he should be asking her. Not me.

And if he's asking his wife the questions, there's only one relevant question to ask her. Not, "Who's this guy?" Or, "How long has this been going on?"

The only question that matters, the only one she wants to hear?

How can I make you happy?

Gita M. Smith is a former reporter for *The Atlanta Journal-Constitution* and the *Montgomery Advertiser*. She's a founding member of the international flash fiction group, House of Writers. When she is not writing, she reads submissions for *Easy Street* and hosts readings of new work by Alabama writers.

Chuck Taylor

Re-Creation

Why not the garage? You could live in the garage?" She queried. She was in the hall closet, pulling out the vacuum cleaner. He was in the living room.

"No," Charley said. "The garage is full."

"If you organized."

"Why don't you live in the garage?

"I take care of the children, remember?"

"It's dirty."

"Sweep. Get a carpet."

"With an RV I can cook. I'd have a bathroom. Air conditioning."

"If we could afford an RV, we could afford to separate."

She was in the kitchen now. She pulled a knife from the drawer and fetched carrots from the fridge and started cutting them into pieces on the cutting board.

He walked to the far side of the living room and started poking at ashes in the fireplace. Here it was July and he hadn't cleaned out the fireplace since the last time they had a fire, Christmas Eve when they opened presents. It had been a long time since he felt like keeping up with chores around the house.

"I'm not the one who went out and got laid." It came out of his mouth without thinking.

The rhythm of chopping broke for a moment.

"But you wanted to. It was always in your eyes."

"So, you read minds now? Why don't you start a home business and bring in some money reading minds? Then I wouldn't need to do so many long hauls in the truck."

His wife Marie continued chopping and did not answer.

"I'm going," he finally said. He went out the back door. He got the leash off the hook from the garage and took his Collie out the side gate in the backyard. They walked north four blocks, until they reached the Wal-Mart parking lot.

The sun was going down. The sky to the west was beginning to turn yellow and red, but the RV's chrome still gleamed.

He walked around the vehicle checking the tires. He went inside and opened windows to air the place out. It was a used RV, but he'd had it checked out by a mechanic who said it was good. The price was a reasonable three thousand. That left Marie with two thousand in the bank and he had two thousand stashed in the RV.

He started up the RV and headed for Highway 21. The collie sat in the seat next to him. She always enjoyed going places. He was headed west. How far he did not know.

He thought about the kids. Would they understand? Most likely not. How could they? How could they know he was dead inside; that he needed to leave to save what life he had left? Tears were in his eyes, but he kept going.

He knew the farther he got from Marie and the kids the stronger he'd feel a tug in his heart. He did not know if the tug would get strong enough to get him to turn around. The collie looked up at him.

"Don't judge," he said. "Don't judge."

Chuck Taylor won the Austin Book Award for his work, *What Do You Want, Blood?* He worked as a poet-in-residence for the City of Salt Lake, was a part-owner of Paperback Plus in Austin, has operated *Slough Press* for 41 years, teaches creative writing at Texas A&M/College Station, and has published novels, books of poetry, and memoirs.

Find out more at: www.facebook.com/chucktaylorallstarshoesnot/

Rise and Shine © Olga S. Jasper

Judith Lessler

Grandmother Bell Puts Alex to Bed

Alex's parents went to Africa for a week to work, so Grandmother Bell went to Baltimore to care for her grandson. The days went well. But bedtime? Not so well.

When Alex's parents returned, Grandmother tells them, "The bedtime routine is now a three-act play."

"Oh," her son says. "Didn't we warn you he would try to add things?"

"You did," says Grandmother. "He's a master. It started Sunday, the first night you were away."

She explained. When Grandmother said it was bath time, Alex refused and started to cry, wail really. As an experienced parent of five, she recognized the beginnings of a full-scale temper-tantrum complete with flinging the body to the floor, turning red, kicking and flailing, and the holding of one's breath. She quickly ran and grabbed the three Lego figures they had played with earlier, named Pretend Alex, Pretend Anya, and Pretend Maria, after Alex and his real-life friends.

She bounced them up and down and said in pretend friend voices, "Alex, we're dirty. Please, please let us take a bath with you."

It worked! Off they went to execute the existing routine—select PJs and clothes for the next day; bathe, brush teeth, put on PJs; descend to the living room to listen to classical music by calling out. "Echo. Play Beethoven's Für Elise." Then up to the bedroom for stories, a kiss, and a hug.

"I dimmed the lights for Beethoven," Grandmother reports. "That's now a requirement."

"OK, that's easy" says her son. "But, what's the three-act play?"

"I've written it down for you," Grandmother says. "I can explain the reason behind everything."

She hands her son the script, and he reads it aloud.

ACT I, Scene 1. Enter the bedroom, choose the PJs, and put out four outfits: 1) shorts, short-sleeved shirt, underwear, and socks for a warm day, 2) some long pants and shirt for a cool day, 3) and 4) a second version of each in case it rains.

Grandmother's daughter-in-law asks, "How so?"

"On Tuesday, I mentioned it might be cool Wednesday," Grandmother replies.

"And that it might rain?" asks her son.

"I mentioned that on Thursday."

"I see," he replies, and continues reading.

ACT I, Scene 2. Take the three pretend friends into the bath. Alex will make each a pretend birthday cake. Use the correct voices for each pretend friend to thank Alex for the cakes.

"I can demonstrate the voices and the correct phrases," she says.

He pauses, and Grandmother asks, "Want to practice now?"

They don't.

ACT I, Scene 3. Towel Game. After drying Alex and his friends, wrap Alex in a towel. Alex will march through the bedroom chugging and tooting, pretending to be a train. Follow along making caboose whistles. Game is over when towel falls off. No matter what he says, there is only ONE towel game. Put on PJs and brush teeth.

"Do we need to brush the teeth of the Lego Kids?" her son asks.

"No," said Grandmother. "He says they don't have teeth."

Son and daughter-in-law giggle, but read on.

Intermission. Descend to living room for music.

ACT II. Your Echo device can play two versions of Für Elise, a quiet one that Alex likes and a loud one that Pretend Alex likes. Play both. Dim the lights, snuggle next to Alex, cradle Lego friends on your forearm, and callout the instruction to Echo. You will have to experiment with the intonation and may end up listening to the quiet or loud version a few times before you get the right version.

Son and daughter-in-law look at Grandmother with raised eyebrows.

"He said, 'Don't interrupt Beethoven.'"

Son and daughter-in-law laugh out loud.

Intermission: Return to bedroom.

Act III. In the bedroom. Sit on the bed with Alex and arrange the three pretend friends so they all can see the book. Let Alex choose pages for each amigo to read. Use the same voices you used to thank him for the cakes.

"That's it?" her son asks.

"Not exactly," the grandmother says. "I know you said I should, but I did not leave the room after the stories. I laid down and told him about your day in Africa, how you loved and missed him, how excited you would be to fly home to see him, and what we would eat for breakfast. Then, we slept together for a while."

Grandmother's son and daughter-in-law are quiet for a moment; she waits to be scolded for breaking their routine.

"Thanks, Mom, for taking such good care of Alex."

Judith T. Lessler is an organic farmer and writes a weekly column for the Durham Farmers' Market Newsletter entitled *Missives from a Market Farmer*. She has published three short pieces in *The Sun's Readers Write* section, two ekphratic poems in a local publication, *Vision and Voice*, and a short personal essay, *Doors and Windows*, in the *Dead Mule School for Southern Literature.*

Visit Judy at www.harlands-creek-farm.com.

Gregg Cusick
Ojos y Risas

(Eyes and Laughter)

The most crucial element of their van, Carlos believes, is, of course, the wall-mounted fans, one on each end of the tiny space inside, they blow enough so that where they meet—where Carlos preps the tacos and burritos and wraps the tamales—is the confluence of cool streams in his desert. His father, Pepe, would disagree, saying most important is, of course, Carlos' mother's tamales. And the tamale sauce she claims has special and secret ingredients, including parts of chickens that no one who bought from their food truck would knowingly eat. Pepe winks at Carlos, alluding to these ingredients and saying no one knows but himself and Carlos' mother. But Rosa winks at Carlos and in this way tells him that his father is wrong.

Everything in Carlos' parents' lives has been difficult, and while his mother's eyes will smile, either with such winks—or broader, green and flashing, mischievous, which Carlos loves the most—his mother never laughs. Because his father never laughs. Because laughter is an expression of overconfidence, of *superioridad*, Pepe tells his son. As if you are better than others and you are, what, making joke of them. Carlos doesn't know what to think because he deeply wants to laugh, like his classmates at the MLK Middle School in town, with whom he sometimes lets out an involuntary chuckle. And what if the joke is on you, he wants to ask his father, what then? Is it okay to laugh, then, at yourself? But Pepe would probably say that there was not such a situation, or you should never put yourself in one.

And so Carlos doesn't, at least not until the day the gringo comes to the window, a day when the outside temperature is mid-90s and humid, too, as Carlos' classmates like to add, as if that makes it worse still. Although from the inside of the van with cooking all around him and the air stifling as the inside of a furniture mover's truck like his parents had crossed the border in and nearly died (one in their small group, a cousin, had perished on the journey,) Carlos wonders if the surface of the sun is humid and, if so, could it be hotter than it already is? (No, he thinks again: his mother's tamales are important, but the fans most crucial.)

So the gringo steps to the window, angles in front of a family of four dressed and coming from church, and Rosa overhears him muttering something about ICE and "Sending you home." Drunk, he's probably lazy, too, Carlos thinks, his eyes smiling at these ideas that people believe about his family and other Hispanics. The gringo's shiny, fleshy face fills the window, and Rosa can smell him over her cooking, a blend of sweat, whiskey, and stale smoke from the Marlboro Reds outlined in his shirt pocket. He orders four tamales and says, "Give me some hot sauce on those." Which means Carlos will have to unwrap the corn husks he folded so neatly.

The gringo reaches onto the windowsill for the red squeeze bottle, drips a quarter-sized dollop onto the back of his paw. Licks it and grumbles, "Not this weak shit, something really hot I know you got it."

Carlos, unrolling the tamales on the narrow counter, glances across at his mother and his father. Pepe, too, looks to Rosa, his expression almost hopeful, Carlos thinks. The slightest of nods from her and Carlos reaches to the high shelf for an unmarked yellow bottle.

Carlos squeezes a generous amount of the rust-colored liquid onto the four tamales laid out before him, then a little more for good measure. Rosa watches, her face without expression, her eyes the only indicator. Carlos then smoothly re-folds the tamales in their husks and bags them. Hands the bag to Rosa who takes the gringo's twenty, hands it to Pepe who makes change.

Rosa's eyes now show something like amusement. And when the gringo shuffles away, Rosa looks right and left at her husband and son, then to the neatly dressed man and his family who have patiently waited and taken in the whole exchange. Rosa's eyes flash and ignite what is her first, an explosion of laughter, which quickly spreads to the others.

Gregg Cusick's short story collection, *My Father Moves Through Time Like a Dirigible,* was published by Livingston Press in 2014. He lives in Durham, North Carolina, where he bartends and tutors literacy.

Marisa Moks-Unger
The Dance

Gus danced with all the dames. He loved swing best. He began with East Coast Swing. Then, he hopped to the cool moves of West Coast Swing.

He knew ballroom, too: waltz, foxtrot, and rumba. Had Sister Immaculata to thank for that. She taught ballroom at St. Joseph's Orphanage. Gus fondly remembered dancing with the Riley twins, Diana and Donna. Unlike Gus, who was a resident until the day he graduated and left for basic training, the Riley girls were adopted at age eight.

He thought both girls were dolls, but had an odd pang in his heart each time he held hands on the dance floor with Donna. Looking her in the eyes made his heart pound harder. It was for that reason Gus concentrated on the beauty mark under her left eye. On the autumn day when they left, a hard downpour came outside. And it rained in Gus's heart that day, too, as he watched Donna and Diana leave with their new family.

Gus was a prodigy and would have made a swell formal dance instructor himself. Sister Immaculata said so! She was convinced of his talents early on. As he grew during his early teens, Gus became an assistant dance partner in class.

Decades later, he went to monthly dances at the VFW halls. Gus, who had never married, attended alone. He liked it that way.

He could dance with all the dames.

The open social dance events drew people of all ages to enjoy learning new moves while meeting new friends. One of his newest friends was Rachel, who had recently graduated from college. Her degree was in accounting, but she worked as a wedding planner. Rachel often suggested that clients attend to brush up on their skills before the big day. And Gus was happy to oblige.

Once he danced with a former resident of the orphanage, Roberta, who like Gus, had never married. She had been the care provider for her aunts, uncles, and cousins as they one by one passed on from measles, mumps, and polio. She had told Gus that one of the Riley twins had died, but could not remember which one. This news shook Gus to the core. Had he really missed the chance to dance one last time with Donna?

A few months later, summer gave way into a glorious fall. The leaves shimmered and shone in the sunset as Gus arrived at the monthly dance. The warmer than usual temperatures produced a magical quality to the hall. With the rustling leaves sweeping into the hall from propped open doors, anything seemed possible.

Gus was on the dance floor with Flo, a receptionist at Dr. DeMarus's office. While he was doing a lindy hop with Flo, they both took in the large group entering the ballroom. A convention of purple hat ladies had arrived in town a day early. And they were all eager to take to the floor to stroll and shag the night away. Gus danced with a dozen—maybe more—of the purple hat dames.

He was heading to the bar to get a whiskey sour when Rachel tapped him on the shoulder.

"I want you to meet my mother, Marie," she proudly told Gus.

"Hi Marie," Gus said, aware that he had met this dame before, but the disco ball's glare prevented him from getting a good look at her. "Can I get you two drinks?"

"Just two waters, thanks," replied Rachel. When Gus returned a few moments later, Rachel was already on the dance floor.

"Dance with me, Marie?"

It was a slow two-step and an easy dance for anyone to follow. Marie nodded and walked onto the dance floor with Gus. They held hands and his heart began to race. It was an old feeling he hadn't experienced in 80-some odd years. As the song ended he drew her into a close embrace, whispering, "You remind me of someone."

Marie drew back, still holding hands.

"Thank you for the dance," she said, smiling softly. As she walked over to Rachel she glanced back at Gus, the beauty mark under her left eye was clearly visible.

He could hear Sister Immaculata's voice, "Donna Marie Riley! You keep that dress clean!"

Gus' eyes locked with Marie's across the dance floor. The warmth of her smile crossed the years between them and he was a boy again; a boy who got to have one more dance with the girl who still held his heart.

Marisa Moks-Unger, Erie County Poet Laureate, (2016-2018) facilitates the *Picture This Project*, including online creative writing workshops that have lead to the *Picture This Anthology*, which she edited. Her work appears in many publications, including *Trust and Trust Regained in Eternal Snow* (Nirala Publications, New Delhi).

Ground Cherry Web © Susan Emshwiller

Suzi Banks Baum
Fresh Greens

Dedicated to my Mom who died on
October 10, 2010 at 6:06 AM

axie's three younger sisters are playing Candy Land at the dining room table. They can keep a game going 'til dark. Mom wipes her hands on her blue striped apron. Maxie watches her slip tennies on and tie the laces snug. She's headed somewhere further than the compost by the bunny cage next to the garden.

"Maxie girl," she calls from the back hallway, "walk with me for dandelions. Hasenpfeffer needs fresh greens."

Maxie rises off the couch, orange plaid indents imprinted on the back of her thighs. Mom hangs her apron on a hook by the back door, heads out.

Looking through the screen door, Maxie watches her mom stand over their homemade fishpond, a 'water feature' the garden catalogues would say. It's an old trough sunk into the grass with herbs planted around. Mom looks proud of her creation, sort of quietly impressed. Five koi pull bright orange stripes around the dark water. Maxie is a little bit proud of her mom too, but also a little bit mad after what happened at the bank this afternoon. She'd never seen Mom so angry.

Her mom made or pretty much invented everything around this house. That apron? One of dad's old shirts, swiveled around, cut off the sleeves, shape a round neck, and voilà, you have an apron. This rug Maxie stands on? Made out of Bunny Bread wrappers and pantyhose bags. Mom hates how everything comes in plastic, so she braids cut strips of the bags into rugs. She is the daughter of a farmer and does almost everything at their house, cleans the chimney, trims the trees, and fixes what's broken. Dad left last summer, so it is up to her. And up to Maxie, now that she is 13, and tall.

This afternoon, Mom picked up Maxie and the girls at the library. Maxie steadied their tower of books under her chin so she could hold her youngest sister's hand in the parking lot. At the bank, the three girls stayed in the car reading. Maxie ran in after Mom. They waited on a leather couch, watching Ludington Street framed by tall velvet curtains. Her boring town looked like a postcard, the Woolworth's decked out for spring. Her mom went into the glass-walled office to talk to a man they knew from church. From where Maxie sat tapping her clogs on the thick rug, she could see Mom's smile sink off her face. She could not hear what the man said, but from the sound of Mom's voice floating into the lobby for everyone to hear, it did not sound good. Her mom clutched her purse; her knuckles got white and her face red. When she came out, she blasted right past. Maxie ran to the car. Mom got in, slammed the door hard, but said nothing. Three sets of brown eyes peered over their books, each filled with questions for Maxie. She shrugged and buckled in.

Maxie stands next to Mom by the fishpond now. They study the tips of green things poking up through last year's leaves. Maxie slips in under Mom's chin, where she fits perfectly and wraps her arms around Mom's waist.

"He cleaned out our savings Maxie," Mom whispers "The money I've been putting aside for summer camp and new shoes for you girls. Gone."

Maxie peeps down at the small white flowers painted on her wooden clogs. They make her think of Edelweiss in the song Mary Poppins sang. She could wear these shoes forever.

"Where is Dad? Did he come to town to get the money?"

Her mom's breath warms the top of Maxie's head.

She asks again, "Didn't he want to see us?"

"No, my darling."

"Will we get to see him again?"

"I don't know girl. That I do not know."

Mom steps back, and heads to the gate. Once they're both through, she locks the secret latch she's wired to protect the garden from kids who run down the alleyways at night. Maxie knows those teens from the dances at the Civic Center. They ransack people's gardens and get away with it. "All for fun," the silver haired neighbor ladies say and laugh.

Maxie tips up her chin to see the thumbnail moon.

"I see the moon and the moon sees me," Mom says, turning from the gate.

"God bless the moon and God bless me," says Maxie.

Mom grabs her hand and tucks it in the warmth under her arm. Not quite shoulder-to-shoulder, they set off down the alley for dandelions.

Suzi Banks Baum is a writer, artist, actress, teacher, community organizer, and mom. She grew up in Michigan's Upper Peninsula, lives in the Berkshires of western Massachusetts, and teaches in the U.S. and Armenia. Suzi uses words, hand bound books, and photographs to say what she means.

ABOUT THE PHOTOGRAPHERS

Anne Anthony's photographs have been published as cover art for *Bartleby Snopes and Crack the Spine.* The Chatham County Agricultural & Conference Center selected her photo, *King of the Roost*, to be featured in their 2017 Grand Opening Celebration.

Jacqueline Anthony is a recent transplant to Vermont from the DC Area. Accompanied by her two pups and a camera, she enjoys exploring her new surroundings and finding beauty in every day.

Suzi Banks Baum is a writer, artist, actress, teacher, community organizer, and mom. She grew up in Michigan's Upper Peninsula, lives in the Berkshires of western Massachusetts, and teaches in the U.S. and Armenia. Suzi uses words, hand bound books, and photographs to say what she means. More at www.suzibanksbaum.com.

Nena Callaghan has a B.S. in Elementary Education and a B.A. in English Literature from Fayetteville State University. Her work appeared in *Bursting Plethora, The Red Line Magazine*, and *The Caribbean Writer*, a publication of the University of the Virgin Islands. Her photographs have appeared in *Glint Literary Journal*.

Patricia Decker has been shooting photographs for years. She admires writers, the other half of the brain, however, finds the strongest way to communicate is with a camera and has made it her profession. An effective photo tells a story in one glance and she loves telling the stories. See her photography at: patriciadecker.smugmug.com

Susan Emshwiller is a produced screenwriter (co-writer of the film "Pollock"), filmmaker, published playwright and short story writer. Recent or upcoming publications include *The Magazine of Fantasy and Science Fiction, Dramatists Play Service, Independent Ink, Gone Lawn, and Black Heart Magazine.* She teaches screenwriting at North Carolina State University.

Judy Guenther, a fine art photographer, captures landscapes, people, places, architecture, and street scenes as she travels the world. She is a member of The Art League at the Torpedo Arts Center in Alexandria, VA, the Northern Virginia Photographic Society, and the F11 Women's Photography Collective. Her photographs have been displayed nationally. Learn more: www.judyguentherphotography.com.

Samantha Hess graduated from UNC Wilmington with a BS degree in Biology. She now resides in Chapel Hill where she enjoys hiking and visits to her local coffee haunts and taking photos while doing both. Follow her on Instagram @samantharuthh.

Olga Jasper is originally from Kyiv (Kiev), Ukraine, now based in Elizabeth City, the USA. She's worked as a photographer in Ukraine and Jordan, and now she is busy in establishing herself in photography in the United States.

Rollin Jewett, an award winning playwright, screenwriter, singer/songwriter, and actor, has feature film credits which include "Laws of Deception" and "American Vampire". His award-winning plays have been produced all over the world. Mr. Jewett lives in Holly Springs, NC with his wife and son. His photographs are available for sale here: fineartamerica.com/profiles/rollin-jewett.html.

Angela Kubinec lives and writes in South Carolina. She is a Senior Editor at *Easy Street Magazine*, an online literary journal.

Tricia Leaf lives in Durham, NC with her husband, two sons, and wild dog. In-between stepping on Legos, attending soccer games, and grading papers, she tries to create images, in words and photos. She is working on a memoir and recently published a flash nonfiction excerpt, *Three Minutes* in *Word Riot*.

Stephen James Moore was born in Hertfordshire, United Kingdom; studied in Newcastle Upon Tyne and Brighton and now lives and writes in Bristol, UK. He works in a cardiac catheterisation suite. He enjoys film, photography, running and literature. He also enjoys beatnik-urban-voodoo. View his Instagram photos @stephen_james_moore.

Brittany Murdock is a New York native, currently residing in Raleigh, who is a writer and social media coordinator of two local magazines. She loves exploring new restaurants around the triangle area and spending time with her family and friends. View her photographs on Instagram @britmurds.

Christine Paris, a member of *Arts Council of Windsor,* exhibits her photographs and artwork with them. She's donated to the Yoga4Hope benefiting Pajama Angels, a not-for-profit for all cancers and chronic diseases. She recently published a children's book series with Austin Macauley Publishing. *Gaia's Journey* will be released in 2018. Her artwork is available online at christine-paris.pixels.com or on Facebook, Serenity Song Designs.

Jen Puchala, a Suffolk Law School graduate, lives in New England and enjoys taking photographs to capture the less hectic moments outside the office. Her favorite subjects are her two dogs, Sage and Sydney, who she pampers at every turn. Follow her on Instagram: @Jennifer_puchala_photography.

ABOUT THE COVER ART

The artwork gracing the front cover is an unfinished painting by Marilyn Penrod, an artist of The Joyful Jewel who parted this life in 2016. She described her painting style as "Domestic Expressionism" and wrote that she "Painted simple scenes of everyday life and used vibrant color to express her emotional connection with them."

The cover art depicts her comfortable chair set in the corner of her own living room where she'd often read a book late into the evening. Those who knew her well also knew how she enjoyed her stash of chocolates hidden in the table drawer beside her.

Visit her artistic legacy: www.marilynpenrod.com.

ABOUT THE EDITORS

Anne Anthony holds a Masters in Professional Writing from Carnegie Mellon University. Her poetry and fiction has been published in the *Dead Mule School for Southern Literature, Poetry South,* and elsewhere. She lives and writes full-time in North Carolina.

Learn more: anneanthony.weebly.com.

Photograph credit: Tracy Huffman Photography

Cathleen O'Connor PhD, writer, speaker, teacher, coach and intuitive, offers editing, publishing, book-layout and marketing services to writers. She is co-author of the bestselling book, *365 Days of Angel Prayers,* has been quoted in the *Huffington Post* and blogs regularly.

Learn more: www.cathleenoconnor.com

"Whenever you read a good book,
somewhere in the world
a door opens to allow
in more light."
—Vera Nazarian

Made in the USA
Columbia, SC
31 March 2018